THE DAWN OF DEATH

Dawn was spreading whitely over the eastern hills when Kane woke. He turned his face again to the hills. Along that grim skyline dwelt some evil foe to the sons of men, and that mere fact was as much a challenge to the Puritan as had ever been a glove thrown in his face by some hot-headed gallant of Devon.

Up the slopes he went, halting a moment to gaze back over the way he had come.

And while he gazed, with a sudden rush of grisly wings the terror was upon him! Kane whirled, galvanized. Kane saw a spread of mighty wings, from which glared a horribly human face. Then he drew and fired...

Bantam Science Fiction and Fantasy
Ask your bookseller for the books you have missed

CONAN THE SWORDSMAN by L. Sprague de Camp,
   Lin Carter and Bjorn Nyberg
CONAN THE LIBERATOR by L. Sprague de Camp
   and Lin Carter
KULL by Robert E. Howard
SOLOMON KANE: SKULLS IN THE STARS
   by Robert E. Howard
SOLOMON KANE: THE HILLS OF THE DEAD
   by Robert E. Howard

#2
SOLOMON KANE

The Hills of the Dead

BY ROBERT E. HOWARD

Introduction by Ramsey Campbell

RL 9, IL 8-up

SOLOMON KANE #2: THE HILLS OF THE DEAD
A Bantam Book / March 1979

Map by Tim Kirk

All rights reserved.
Copyright © 1979 by Alla Ray Kuykendall
and Alla Ray Morris
Cover art copyright © 1979 by Bantam Books, Inc.

ACKNOWLEDGMENTS

The Hills of the Dead, copyright 1930 by Popular Fiction Publishing Company for Weird Tales, August 1930.
Part of Hawk of Basti originally appeared in Red Shadows, copyright © 1968 by Glenn Lord. The complete version appears here for the first time.
The Return of Sir Richard Grenville, copyright © 1968 by Glenn Lord for Red Shadows.
Wings in the Night, copyright 1932 by Popular Fiction Publishing Company for Weird Tales, July 1932.
The Footfalls Within, copyright 1931 by Popular Fiction Publishing Company for Weird Tales, September 1931.
Part of The Children of Asshur originally appeared in Red Shadows, copyright © 1968 by Glenn Lord. The complete version appears here for the first time.
Solomon Kane's Homecoming, copyright 1936 by Shephered & Wollheim for Fanciful Tales, Fall 1936.

This book may not be reproduced in whole or in part, by mimeograph or any other means, without permission.
For information address: Bantam Books, Inc.

ISBN 0-553-12166-9

Published simultaneously in the United States and Canada

Bantam Books are published by Bantam Books, Inc. Its trademark, consisting of the words "Bantam Books" and the portrayal of a bantam, is Registered in U.S. Patent and Trademark Office and in other countries. Marca Registrada. Bantam Books, Inc., 666 Fifth Avenue, New York, New York 10019.

PRINTED IN THE UNITED STATES OF AMERICA

CONTENTS

THE MYSTERY OF SOLOMON KANE by Ramsey Campbell	ix
THE HILLS OF THE DEAD	1
HAWK OF BASTI	24
THE RETURN OF SIR RICHARD GRENVILLE	48
WINGS IN THE NIGHT	50
THE FOOTFALLS WITHIN	86
THE CHILDREN OF ASSHUR	104
SOLOMON KANE'S HOMECOMING	139

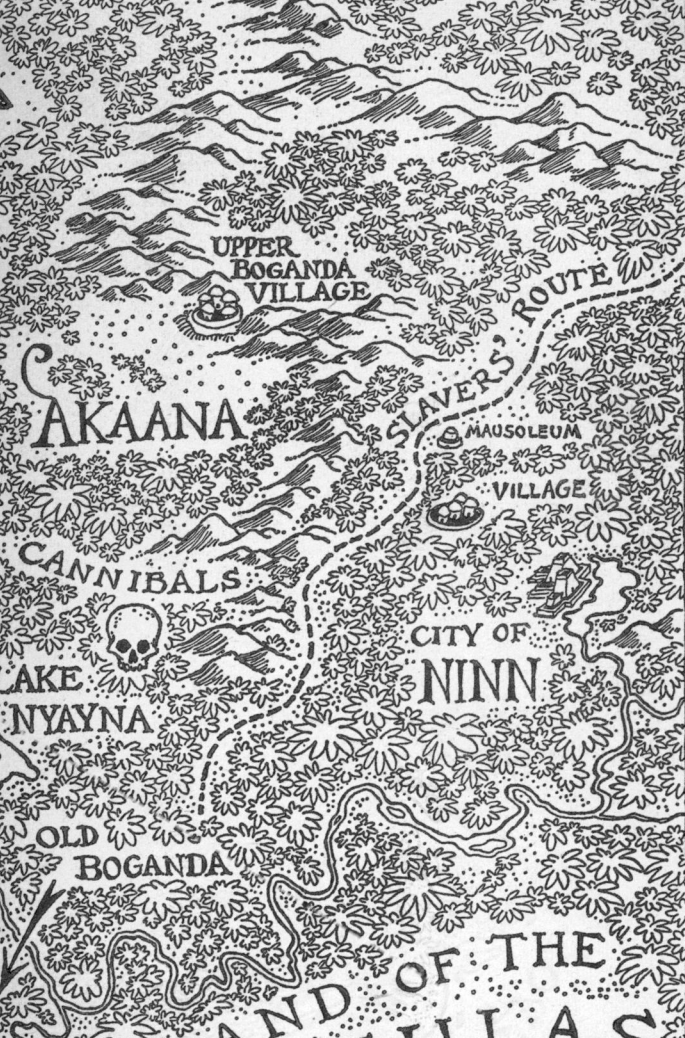

The Mystery of
SOLOMON KANE

by Ramsey Campbell

Perhaps this book ought to begin with Sir Richard Grenville.

He might almost have been a Robert E. Howard character himself. A cousin of Sir Francis Drake, he was an obsessive voyager. He planted the first English colony in America in 1584. Ten years earlier, he had planned a voyage to discover *Terra Australis*, a surmised continent in the southern hemisphere; but Queen Elizabeth refused him the license, on the basis that it was not the time to challenge the Spanish Empire, and granted it to Drake three years later.

It must have been the story of the *Revenge* which most appealed to Howard. In 1591, a small squadron of six English vessels was sent to wait at the Azores for the Spanish treasure fleet. They were attacked by twenty galleons of the Spanish navy. Five of the vessels ran; but Grenville fought, even though sickness had left only ninety of the crew of the *Revenge* fit for action. He fought for fifteen hours; while the *Revenge* was riddled with eight hundred cannonballs, it sank two Spanish ships.

The Spanish recognized his valor, and offered him terms of surrender: he and his officers would be held in honorable captivity for ransom, the common seamen would not be set to row galleys but would be given safe passage to England. Even this was not enough for Grenville, who seems to have been as much of an atavism as Kane. Apparently in a spirit of "death before dishonor," he ordered the *Revenge* to be blown up. He was overborne, and died on the Spanish flagship of his wounds—or, as the legend tells, he chewed fragments of a wine goblet in order to end his life.

It seems that Kane was there; he addresses Grenville's ghost as "long fallen at my side." This is worth remembering—for it is one of the few facts we have about Solomon Kane.

We know he "was not wholly a Puritan." Since the term "Puritan" was so variously applied, that statement is more vague than it may seem. However, Howard conveys a sense of the man himself that accumulates throughout the tales, and that need not be summarized here. We know also that Kane had unchronicled adventures—when did he suffer "scars made by Moslem whips in a Turkish galley"? But intentionally or not, this helps to make Kane a mysterious figure.

Even his dates are conjectural. Commentators have assumed that "Solomon Kane's Homecoming" takes place in 1610 on the basis that Bess, who has been dead for seven years, is Queen Elizabeth; I assumed so myself. But is this likely? One historian describes the Queen as "a huge boulder in the path of Puritanism, unavoidable, insurmountable, immovable." The Puritan ideal was to make oneself clear to the common people; Elizabeth was hostile to preaching, and more hostile to "prophesyings"—meetings of ministers to discuss the Scriptures—which she saw as a political threat. On matters of church reform she refused to support the Puritans. Many Puritans blamed her advisers rather than the Queen—but not so Solomon Kane, to judge from his reaction to her name in "Hawk of Basti." It seems unlikely that he would later say, "Woe that I caused her tears"—and besides, Queen Elizabeth was buried not by the sea but in Westminster Abbey in London. Whoever Bess was, she only adds to the mystery of Kane.

At least we can be reasonably sure of Kane's weapons. His rapier was not the sort to which Errol Flynn has accustomed us, nor would his fencing have been so rapid. Kane's blade would have been diamond-shaped in section, and perhaps more than four feet long; the rapier of that period was blade-heavy. (Blades were shortened for lightness around 1650; about 1670 the section was divided, giving the triangular short-sword blade.) In fencing, opponents generally faced each other rather than turning side on. There was relatively little delicacy; hacking with the blade's edge was more common than thrusting (though Kane favors subtlety and the use of the point). One might use a dagger in conjunction with the rapier, as Kane sometimes does. Incidentally, the fact that Kane's rapier guard is "unadorned" may not be an effect of Puritanism; one trick of swordplay was to insert one's swordpoint amid the decorations of the opponent's cup-guard and disarm him.

The musket which Kane sometimes carries was a cumbersome weapon, slow to use. It may have weighed as much as twenty pounds; its barrel was four feet long. It was designed to penetrate heavy armor, but Kane uses it, when at all, as a bludgeon. His pistols would probably have been snaphaunces— a forerunner of the flintlock, but lacking its safety feature of the half-cock.

These details apart, we must learn about Kane from the stories. In "Blades of the Brotherhood," piracy appears to be flourishing; perhaps this is later than the defeat of the Spanish Armada, so that Kane has already sailed with Grenville. After this brief return to England, we find him next in Africa. On the West Coast, in "Hills of the Dead," he encounters vampirism; he meets an old acquaintance from his seafaring days, *Hawk of Basti*; Sir Richard Grenville appears to him. As he wanders east, he comes upon a city of the inhuman: "Wings in the Night." Further east, menaced by "The Footfalls Within," he discovers an ancient use of the magical staff he carries. Still deeper into the jungle, he discovers the survival of an ancient civilization—"The Children of Asshur."

I have added conclusions to the two unfinished stories, "Hawk of Basti," and "The Children of Asshur." In both, Howard's original work has been left untouched. But no image of mine could so sum up the brooding mystery of Kane as the final poem here, the ironically titled "Solomon Kane's Homecoming." May he and Howard be long remembered.

#2
SOLOMON KANE

The Hills of the Dead

THE HILLS OF THE DEAD

CHAPTER 1
VOODOO

The twigs which N'Longa flung on the fire broke and crackled. The upleaping flames lighted the countenances of the two men. N'Longa, voodoo man of the Slave Coast, was very old. His wizened and gnarled frame was stooped and brittle, his face creased by hundreds of wrinkles. The red firelight glinted on the human finger-bones which composed his necklace.

The other was an Englishman, and his name was Solomon Kane. He was tall and broad-shouldered, clad in black close garments, the garb of the Puritan. His featherless slouch hat was drawn low over his heavy brows, shadowing his darkly pallid face. His cold deep eyes brooded in the firelight.

"You come again, brother," droned the fetish-man, speaking in the jargon which passed for a common language of black man and white on the West Coast. "Many moons burn and die since we make blood-palaver. You go to the setting sun, but you come back!"

"Aye," Kane's voice was deep and almost ghostly. "Yours is a grim land, N'Longa, a red land barred with the black darkness of horror and the bloody shadows of death. Yet I have returned—"

N'Longa stirred the fire, saying nothing, and after a pause Kane continued.

"Yonder in the unknown vastness"—his long finger stabbed at the black silent jungle which brooded beyond the firelight—"yonder lie mystery and adventure and nameless terror. Once I dared the jungle—

1

once she nearly claimed my bones. Something entered into my blood, something stole into my soul like a whisper of unnamed sin. The jungle! Dark and brooding—over leagues of the blue salt sea she has drawn me and with the dawn I go to seek the heart of her. Mayhap I shall find curious adventure—mayhap my doom awaits me. But better death than the ceaseless and ever-lasting urge, the fire that has burned my veins with bitter longing."

"She call," muttered N'Longa. "At night she coil like serpent about my hut and whisper strange things to me. Ai ya! The jungle call. We be blood-brothers, you and I. Me, N'Longa, mighty worker of nameless magic! You go to the jungle as all men go who hear her call. Maybe you live, more like you die. You believe in my fetish work?"

"I understand it not," said Kane grimly, "but I have seen you send your soul forth from your body to animate a lifeless corpse."

"Aye! Me N'Longa, priest of the Black God! Now watch, I make magic."

Kane gazed at the old voodoo man who bent over the fire, making even motions with his hands and mumbling incantations. Kane watched and he seemed to grow sleepy. A mist wavered in front of him, through which he saw dimly the form of N'Longa, etched dark against the flames. Then all faded out.

Kane awoke with a start, hand shooting to the pistol in his belt. N'Longa grinned at him across the flame and there was a scent of early dawn in the air. The fetish-man held a long stave of curious black wood in his hands. This stave was carved in a strange manner, and one end tapered to a sharp point.

"This voodoo staff," said N'Longa, putting it in the Englishman's hand. "Where your guns and long knife fail, this save you. When you want me, lay this on your breast, fold your hands on it and sleep. I come to you in your dreams."

Kane weighed the thing in his hand, highly suspicious of witchcraft. It was not heavy, but seemed as hard as iron. A good weapon at least, he decided. Dawn was just beginning to steal over the jungle and the river.

CHAPTER 2

RED EYES

Solomon Kane shifted his musket from his shoulder and let the stock fall to the earth. Silence lay about him like a fog. Kane's lined face and tattered garments showed the effect of long bush travel. He looked about him.

Some distance behind him loomed the green, rank jungle, thinning out to low shrubs, stunted trees and tall grass. Some distance in front of him rose the first of a chain of bare, somber hills, littered with boulders, shimmering in the merciless heat of the sun. Between the hills and the jungle lay a broad expanse of rough, uneven grasslands, dotted here and there by clumps of thorn-trees.

An utter silence hung over the country. The only sign of life was a few vultures flapping heavily across the distant hills. For the last few days Kane had noticed the increasing number of these unsavory birds. The sun was rocking westward but its heat was in no way abated.

Trailing his musket he started forward slowly. He had no objective in view. This was all unknown country and one direction was as good as another. Many weeks ago he had plunged into the jungle with the assurance born of courage and ignorance. Having by some miracle survived the first few weeks, he was becoming hard and toughened, able to hold his own with any of the grim denizens of the fastness he dared.

As he progressed he noted an occasional lion spoor but there seemed to be no animals in the grasslands— none that left tracks, at any rate. Vultures sat like black, brooding images in some of the stunted trees, and suddenly he saw an activity among them some distance beyond. Several of the dusky birds circled about a clump of high grass, dipping, then rising again. Some beast of prey was defending his kill against them, Kane decided, and wondered at the lack of snarling and roaring which usually accompanied such scenes. His curiosity was roused and he turned his steps in that direction.

At last, pushing through the grass which rose about his shoulders, he saw, as through a corridor walled with the rank waving blades, a ghastly sight. The corpse of a black man lay, face down, and as the Englishman looked, a great dark snake rose and slid away into the grass, moving so quickly that Kane was unable to decide its nature. But it had a weird human-like suggestion about it.

Kane stood over the body, noting that while the limbs lay awry as if broken, the flesh was not torn as a lion or leopard would have torn it. He glanced up at the whirling vultures and was amazed to see several of them skimming along close to the earth, following a waving of the grass which marked the flight of the thing which had presumably slain the black man. Kane wondered what thing the carrion birds, which eat only the dead, were hunting through the grasslands. But Africa is full of never-explained mysteries.

Kane shrugged his shoulders and lifted his musket again. Adventures he had had in plenty since he parted from N'Longa some moons agone, but still that nameless paranoid urge had driven him on and on, deeper and deeper into those trackless ways. Kane could not have analyzed this call; he would have attributed it to Satan, who lures men to their destruction. But it was but the restless turbulent spirit of the adventurer, the wanderer—the same urge which sends the gipsy caravans about the world, which drove the Viking galleys over unknown seas and which guides the flights of the wild geese.

Kane sighed. Here in this barren land seemed

neither food nor water, but he had wearied unto death of the dank, rank venom of the thick jungle. Even a wilderness of bare hills was preferable, for a time at least. He glanced at them, where they lay brooding in the sun, and started forward again.

He held N'Longa's fetish stave in his left hand, and though his conscience still troubled him for keeping a thing so apparently diabolic in nature, he had never been able to bring himself to throw it away.

Now as he went toward the hills, a sudden commotion broke out in the tall grass in front of him, which was, in places, taller than a man. A thin, high-pitched scream sounded and on its heels an earth-shaking roar. The grass parted and a slim figure came flying toward him like a wisp of straw blown on the wind—a brown-skinned girl, clad only in a skirt-like garment. Behind her, some yards away but gaining swiftly, came a huge lion.

The girl fell at Kane's feet with a wail and a sob, and lay clutching at his ankles. The Englishman dropped the voodoo stave, raised his musket to his shoulder and sighted coolly at the ferocious feline face which neared him every instant. Crash! The girl screamed once and slumped on her face. The huge cat leaped high and wildly, to fall and lie motionless.

Kane reloaded hastily before he spared a glance at the form at his feet. The girl lay as still as the lion he had just slain, but a quick examination showed that she had only fainted.

He bathed her face with water from his canteen and presently she opened her eyes and sat up. Fear flooded her face as she looked at her rescuer, and she made to rise.

Kane held out a restraining hand and she cowered down, trembling. The roar of his heavy musket was enough to frighten any native who had never before seen a white man, Kane reflected.

The girl was slim and well-formed. Her nose was straight and thin-bridged. She was a deep brown in color, perhaps with a strong Berber strain.

Kane spoke to her in a river dialect, a simple language he had learned during his wanderings, and she replied haltingly. The inland tribes traded slaves and ivory to the river people and were familiar with their jargon.

"My village is there," she answered Kane's question, pointing to the southern jungle with a slim, rounded arm. "My name is Zunna. My mother whipped me for breaking a cooking-kettle and I ran away because I was angry. I am afraid; let me go back to my mother!"

"You may go," said Kane, "but I will take you, child. Suppose another lion came along? You were very foolish to run away."

She whimpered a little. "Are you not a god?"

"No, Zunna. I am only a man, though the color of my skin is not as yours. Lead me now to your village."

She rose hesitantly, eyeing him apprehensively through the wild tangle of her hair. To Kane she seemed like some frightened young animal. She led the way and Kane followed. She indicated that her village lay to the southeast, and their route brought them nearer to the hills. The sun began to sink and the roaring of lions reverberated over the grasslands. Kane glanced at the western sky; this open country was no place in which to be caught by night. He glanced toward the hills and saw that they were within a few hundred yards of the nearest. He saw what seemed to be a cave.

"Zunna," said he haltingly, "we can never reach your village before nightfall. If we bide here the lions will take us. Yonder is a cavern where we may spend the night—"

She shrank and trembled.

"Not in the hills, master!" she whimpered. "Better the lions!"

"Nonsense!" His tone was impatient; he had had enough of native superstition. "We will spend the night in yonder cave."

She argued no further, but followed him. They went up a short slope and stood at the mouth of the cavern, a small affair, with sides of solid rock and a floor of deep sand.

"Gather some dry grass, Zunna," commanded Kane, standing his musket against the wall at the mouth of the cave, "but go not far away, and listen for lions. I will build here a fire which shall keep us safe from beasts tonight. Bring some grass and any twigs you may find, like a good child, and we will sup. I have dried meat in my pouch and water also."

She gave him a strange, long glance, then turned away without a word. Kane tore up grass near at hand, noting how it was seared and crisp from the sun, and heaping it up, struck flint and steel. Flame leaped up and devoured the heap in an instant. He was wondering how he could gather enough grass to keep a fire going all night, when he was aware that he had visitors.

Kane was used to grotesque sights, but at first glance he started and a slight coldness traveled down his spine. Two men stood before him in silence. They were tall and gaunt and entirely naked. Their skins were a dusty black, tinged with a gray, ashy hue, as of death. Their faces were different from any he had ever seen. The brows were high and narrow, the noses huge and snout-like; the eyes were inhumanly large and inhumanly red. As the two stood there it seemed to Kane that only their burning eyes lived.

He spoke to them, but they did not answer. He invited them to eat with a motion of his hand, and they silently squatted down near the cave mouth, as far from the dying embers of the fire as they could get.

Kane turned to his pouch and began taking out the strips of dried meat which he carried. Once he glanced at his silent guests; it seemed to him that they were watching the glowing ashes of his fire, rather than him.

The sun was about to sink behind the western horizon. A red, fierce glow spread over the grasslands, so that all seemed like a waving sea of blood. Kane knelt over his pouch, and glancing up, saw Zunna come around the shoulder of the hill with her arms full of grass and dry branches.

As he looked, her eyes flared wide; the branches dropped from her arms and her scream knifed the silence, fraught with terrible warning. Kane whirled on his knee. Two great forms loomed over him as he came up with the lithe motion of a springing leopard. The fetish stave was in his hand and he drove it through the body of the nearest foe with a force which sent its sharp point out between the man's shoulders. Then the long, lean arms of the other locked about him, and the two went down together.

The talon-like nails of the stranger were tearing at his face, the hideous red eyes staring into his with a terrible threat, as Kane writhed about and, fending off the clawing hands with one arm, drew a pistol. He pressed the muzzle close against the savage side and pulled the trigger. At the muffled report, the stranger's body jerked to the concussion of the bullet, but the thick lips merely gaped in a horrid grin.

One long arm slid under Kane's shoulders, the other hand gripped his hair. The Englishman felt his head being forced back irresistibly. He clutched at the other's wrists with both hands, but the flesh under his frantic fingers was as hard as wood. Kane's brain was reeling; his neck seemed ready to break with a little more pressure. He threw his body backward with one volcanic effort, breaking the deathly hold. The other was on him, and the talons were clutching again. Kane found and raised the empty pistol, and he felt the man's skull cave in like a shell as he brought down the long barrel with all his strength. And once again the writhing lips parted in fearful mockery.

And now a near panic clutched Kane. What sort of man was this, who still menaced his life with tearing fingers, after having been shot and mortally bludgeoned? No man, surely, but one of the sons of Satan!

At the thought Kane wrenched and heaved explosively, and the close-locked combatants tumbled across the earth to come to a rest in the smoldering ashes before the cave mouth. Kane barely felt the heat, but the mouth of his foe gaped, this time in seeming agony. The frightful fingers loosened their hold and Kane sprang clear.

The savage creature with his shattered skull was rising on one hand and one knee when Kane struck, returning to the attack as a gaunt wolf returns to a wounded bison. From the side he leaped, landing full on the sinewy back, his steely arms seeking and finding a deadly wrestling hold; and as they went to the earth together he broke the other's neck, so that the hideous dead face looked back over one shoulder. The body lay still but to Kane it seemed that it was not dead even then, for the red eyes still burned with their grisly light.

The Englishman turned, to see the girl crouching against the cave wall. He looked for his stave; it lay in a heap of dust, among which were a few moldering bones. He stared, his brain reeling. Then with one stride he caught up the voodoo staff and turned to the fallen man. His face set in grim lines as he raised it; then he drove it through the savage breast. And before his eyes, the great body crumbled, dissolving to dust as he watched horror-struck, even as the first opponent had crumbled when Kane had first thrust the stave.

CHAPTER 3
DREAM MAGIC

"Great God!" whispered Kane. "The men were dead! Vampires! This is Satan's handiwork manifested."

Zunna crawled to his knees and clung there.

"These be walking dead men, master," she whimpered. "I should have warned you."

"Why did they not leap on my back when they first came?" asked he.

"They feared the fire. They were waiting for the embers to die entirely."

"Whence came they?"

"From the hills. Hundreds of their kind swarm among the boulders and caverns of these hills, and they live on human life, for a man they will slay, devouring his ghost as it leaves his quivering body. Aye, they are suckers of souls!

"Master, among the greater of these hills there is a silent city of stone, and in the old times, in the days of my ancestors, these people lived there. They were human, but they were not as we, for they had ruled this land for ages and ages. The ancestors of my people made war on them and slew many, and their magicians made all the dead men as these were. At last all died.

"And for ages have they preyed on the tribes of the jungle, stalking down from the hills at midnight and at sunset to haunt the jungle-way and slay and slay. Men and beasts flee them and only fire will destroy them."

"Here is that which will destroy them," said Kane grimly, raising the voodoo stave. "Black magic must fight black magic, and I know not what spell N'Longa put hereon, but—"

"You are a god," Zunna decided aloud. "No man could overcome two of the walking dead men. Master, can you not lift this curse from my tribe? There is nowhere for us to flee and the monsters slay us at will, catching wayfarers outside the village wall. Death is on this land and we die helpless!"

Deep in Kane stirred the spirit of the crusader, the fire of the zealot—the fanatic who devotes his life to battling the powers of darkness.

"Let us eat," said he; "then we will build a great fire at the cave mouth. The fire which keeps away beasts shall also keep away fiends."

* * *

Later Kane sat just inside the cave, chin rested on clenched fist, eyes gazing unseeingly into the fire. Behind in the shadows, Zunna watched him, awed.

"God of Hosts," Kane muttered, "grant me aid! My hand it is which must lift the ancient curse from this dark land. How am I to fight these dead fiends, who yield not to mortal weapons? Fire will destroy them—a broken neck renders them helpless—the voodoo stave thrust through them crumbles them to dust—but of what avail? How may I prevail against the hundreds who haunt these hills, and to whom human life-essence is Life? Have not—as Zunna says—warriors come against them in the past, only to find them fled to their high-walled city where no man can come against them?"

The night wore on. Zunna slept, her cheek pillowed on her round, girlish arm. The roaring of the lions shook the hills and still Kane sat and gazed broodingly into the fire. Outside, the night was alive with whispers and rustlings and stealthily soft footfalls. And at times Kane, glancing up from his meditations, seemed to catch the gleam of great red eyes beyond the flickering light of the fire.

Gray dawn was stealing over the grasslands when Kane shook Zunna into wakefulness.

"God have mercy on my soul for delving in barbaric magic," said he, "but demonry must be fought with demonry, mayhap. Tend ye the fire and aware me if aught untoward occur."

Kane lay down on his back on the sand floor and laid the voodoo staff on his breast, folding his hands upon it. He fell asleep instantly. And sleeping, he dreamed. To his slumbering self it seemed that he walked through a thick fog and in this fog he met N'Longa, true to life. N'Longa spoke, and the words were clear and vivid, impressing themselves on his consciousness so deeply as to span the gap between sleeping and waking.

"Send this girl to her village soon after sunup when the lions have gone to their lairs," said N'Longa, "and bid her bring her lover to you at this cave. There make him lie down as if to slumber, holding the voodoo stave."

The dream faded and Kane awoke suddenly, wondering. How strange and vivid had been the vision, and how strange to hear N'Longa talking in English, without the jargon! Kane shrugged his shoulders. He knew that N'Longa claimed to possess the power of sending his spirit through space, and he himself had seen the voodoo man animate a dead man's body. Still—

"Zunna," said Kane, giving the problem up, "I will go with you as far as the edge of the jungle and you must go on to your village and return here to this cave with your lover."

"Kran?" she asked naively.

"Whatever his name is. Eat and we will go."

Again the sun slanted toward the west. Kane sat in the cave, waiting. He had seen the girl safely to the place where the jungle thinned to the grasslands, and though his conscience stung him at the thought of the dangers which might confront her, he sent her on alone and returned to the cave. He sat now, wondering if he would not be damned to everlasting flames for tinkering with the magic of a black sorcerer, blood-brother or not.

Light footfalls sounded, and as Kane reached for his musket, Zunna entered, accompanied by a tall, splendidly proportioned youth whose brown skin showed that he was of the same race as the girl. His soft dreamy eyes were fixed on Kane in a sort of awesome worship. Evidently the girl had not minimized this new god's glory in her telling.

He bade the youth lie down as he directed and placed the voodoo stave in his hands. Zunna crouched at one side, wide-eyed. Kane stepped back, half ashamed of this mummery and wondering what, if anything, would come of it. Then to his horror, the youth gave one gasp and stiffened!

Zunna screamed, bounding erect.

"You have killed Kran!" she shrieked, flying at the Englishman who stood struck speechless.

Then she halted suddenly, wavered, drew a hand languidly across her brow—she slid down to lie with her arms about the motionless body of her lover.

And this body moved suddenly, made aimless motions with hands and feet, then sat up, disengaging itself from the clinging arms of the still senseless girl.

Kran looked up at Kane and grinned, a sly, knowing grin which seemed out of place on his face somehow. Kane started. Those soft eyes had changed in expression and were now hard and glittering and snaky—N'Longa's eyes!

"Ai ya," said Kran in a grotesquely familiar voice. "Blood-brother, you got no greeting for N'Longa?"

Kane was silent. His flesh crawled in spite of himself. Kran rose and stretched his arms in an unfamiliar sort of way, as if his limbs were new to him. He slapped his breast approvingly.

"Me N'Longa!" said he in the old boastful manner. "Mighty ju-ju man! Blood-brother, not you know me, eh?"

"You are Satan," said Kane sincerely. "Are you Kran or are you N'Longa?"

"Me N'Longa," assured the other. "My body sleep in ju-ju hut on Coast many treks from here. I borrow Kran's body for while. My ghost travel ten days march in one breath; twenty days march in same time. My ghost go out from my body and drive out Kran's."

"And Kran is dead?"

"No, he no dead. I send his ghost to shadow-land for a while—send the girl's ghost too, to keep him company; bimeby come back."

"This is the work of the Devil," said Kane frankly, "but I have seen you do even fouler magic—shall I call you N'Longa or Kran?"

"Kran—bah! Me N'Longa—bodies like clothes! Me N'Longa, in here now!" he rapped his breast. "Bimeby Kran live along here—then he be Kran and I be N'Longa, same like before. Kran no live along now; N'Longa live along this one fellow body. Blood-brother, I am N'Longa!"

Kane nodded. This was in truth a land of horror and enchantment; anything was possible, even that the thin voice of N'Longa should speak to him from the great chest of Kran, and the snaky eyes of N'Longa should blink at him from the handsome young face of Kran.

"This land I know long time," said N'Longa, getting down to business. "Mighty ju-ju, these dead people! No need to waste one fellow time—I know—I talk to you in sleep. My blood-brother want to kill out these dead fellows, eh?"

"'Tis a thing opposed to nature," said Kane somberly. "They are known in my land as vampires—I never expected to come upon a whole nation of them."

CHAPTER 4

THE SILENT CITY

"Now we find this stone city," said N'Longa.

"Yes? Why not send your ghost out to kill these vampires?" Kane asked idly.

"Ghost got to have one fellow body to work in," N'Longa answered. "Sleep now. Tomorrow we start."

The sun had set; the fire glowed and flickered in the cave mouth. Kane glanced at the still form of the girl, who lay where she had fallen, and prepared himself for slumber.

"Awake me at midnight," he admonished, "and I will watch from then until dawn."

But when N'Longa finally shook his arm, Kane awoke to see the first light of dawn reddening the land.

"Time we start," said the fetish-man.

"But the girl—are you sure she lives?"

"She live, blood-brother."

"Then in God's name, we can not leave her here at

the mercy of any prowling fiend who might chance upon her. Or some lion might—"

"No lion come. Vampire scent still linger, mixed with man scent. One fellow lion he no like man scent and he fear the walking dead men. No beast come, and"—lifting the voodoo stave and laying it across the cave entrance—"no dead man come now."

Kane watched him somberly and without enthusiasm.

"How will that rod safeguard her?"

"That mighty ju-ju," said N'Longa. "You see how one fellow vampire go along dust alongside that stave! No vampire dare touch or come near it. I give it to you, because outside Vampire Hills one fellow man sometimes meet a corpse walking in jungle when shadows be black. Not all walking dead men be here. And all must suck Life from men—if not, they rot like dead wood."

"Then make many of these rods and arm the people with them."

"No can do!" N'Longa's skull shook violently. "That ju-ju rod be mighty magic! Old, old! No man live today can tell how old that fellow ju-ju stave be. I make my blood-brother sleep and do magic with it to guard him, that time we make palaver in Coast village. Today we scout and run; no need it. Leave it here to guard girl."

Kane shrugged his shoulders and followed the fetish-man, after glancing back at the still shape which lay in the cave. He would never have agreed to leave her so casually, had he not believed in his heart that she was dead. He had touched her, and her flesh was cold.

They went up among the barren hills as the sun was rising. Higher they climbed, up steep clay slopes, winding their way through ravines and between great boulders. The hills were honeycombed with dark, forbidding caves, and these they passed warily, and Kane's flesh crawled as he thought of the grisly occupants therein. For N'Longa said:

"Them vampires, he sleep in caves most all day till sunset. Them caves, he be full of one fellow dead man."

The sun rose higher, baking down on the bare slopes with an intolerable heat. Silence brooded like an evil monster over the land. They had seen nothing, but Kane could have sworn at times that a black shadow drifted behind a boulder at their approach.

"Them vampires, they stay hid in daytime," said N'Longa with a low laugh. "They be afraid of one fellow vulture! No fool vulture! He knows death when he see it! He pounce on one fellow dead man and tear and eat if he be lying or walking!"

A strong shudder shook his companion.

"Great God!" Kane cried, striking his thigh with his hat; "is there no end to the horror of this hideous land? Truly this land is dedicated to the powers of darkness!"

Kane's eyes burned with a dangerous light. The terrible heat, the solitude and the knowledge of the horrors lurking on either hand were shaking even his steely nerves.

"Keep on one fellow hat, blood-brother," admonished N'Longa with a low gurgle of amusement. "That fellow sun, he knock you dead, suppose you no look out."

Kane shifted the musket he had insisted on bringing and made no reply. They mounted an eminence at last and looked down on a sort of plateau. And in the center of this plateau was a silent city of gray and crumbling stone. Kane was smitten by a sense of incredible age as he looked! The walls and houses were of great stone blocks, yet they were falling into ruin. Grass grew on the plateau, and high in the streets of that dead city. Kane saw no movement among the ruins.

"That is their city—why do they choose to sleep in the caves?"

"Maybe-so one fellow stone fall on them from roof and crush. Them stone huts, he fall down bimeby.

Maybe-so they no like to stay together—maybe-so they eat each other, too."

"Silence!" whispered Kane; "how it hangs over all!"

"Them vampires no talk nor yell; they dead. They sleep in caves, wander at sunset and at night. Maybe-so them fellow bush tribes come with spears, them vampires go to stone kraal and fight behind walls."

Kane nodded. The crumbling walls which surrounded that dead city were still high and solid enough to resist the attack of spearmen—especially when defended by these snout-nosed fiends.

"Blood-brother," said N'Longa solemnly, "I have mighty magic thought! Be silent a little while."

Kane seated himself on a boulder and gazed broodingly at the bare crags and slopes which surrounded them. Far away to the south he saw the leafy green ocean that was the jungle. Distance lent a certain enchantment to the scene. Closer at hand loomed the dark blotches that were the mouths of the caves of horror.

N'Longa was squatting, tracing some strange pattern in the clay with a dagger point. Kane watched him, thinking how easy they might fall victim to the vampire if even three or four of the fiends should come out of their caverns. And even as he thought it, a black and horrific shadow fell across the crouching fetish-man.

Kane acted without conscious thought. He shot from the boulder where he sat like a stone hurled from a catapult, and his musket stock shattered the face of the hideous thing who had stolen upon them. Back and back Kane drove his inhuman foe staggering, never giving him time to halt or launch an offensive, battering him with the onslaught of a frenzied tiger.

At the very edge of the cliff the vampire wavered, then pitched back over, to fall for a hundred feet and lie writhing on the rocks of the plateau below. N'Longa was on his feet pointing; the hills were giving up their dead.

Out of the caves they were swarming, the terrible black silent shapes; up the slopes they came charging and over the boulders they came clambering, and their red eyes were all turned toward the two humans who stood above the silent city. The caves belched them forth in an unholy judgment day.

N'Longa pointed to a crag some distance away and with a shout started running fleetly toward it. Kane followed. From behind boulders taloned hands clawed at them, tearing their garments. They raced past caves, and mummied monsters came lurching out of the dark, gibbering silently, to join in the pursuit.

The dead hands were close at their back when they scrambled up the last slope and stood on a ledge which was at the top of the crag. The fiends halted silently a moment, then came clambering after them. Kane clubbed his musket and smashed down into the red-eyed faces, knocking aside the upleaping hands. They surged up like a great wave; he swung his musket in a silent fury that matched theirs. The wave broke and wavered back; came on again.

He—could—not—kill—them! These words beat on his brain like a sledge on an anvil as he shattered wood-like flesh and dead bone with his smashing swings. He knocked them down, hurled them back, but they rose and came on again. This could not last —what in God's name was N'Longa doing? Kane spared one swift, tortured glance over his shoulder. The fetish-man stood on the highest part of the ledge, head thrown back, arms lifted as if in invocation.

Kane's vision blurred to the sweep of hideous faces with red, staring eyes. Those in front were horrible to see now, for their skulls were shattered, their faces caved in and their limbs broken. But still they came on and those behind reached across their shoulders to clutch at the man who defied them.

Kane was red but the blood was all his. From the long-withered veins of those monsters no single drop of warm red blood trickled. Suddenly from behind him came a long piercing wail—N'Longa! Over the crash of the flying musket-stock and the shattering of bones it sounded high and clear—the only voice lifted in that hideous fight.

The wave of vampires washed about Kane's feet, dragging him down. Keen talons tore at him, flaccid lips sucked at his wounds. He reeled up again, disheveled and bloody, clearing a space with a shattering sweep of his splintered musket. Then they closed in again and he went down.

"This is the end!" he thought, but even at that instant the press slackened and the sky was suddenly filled with the beat of great wings.

Then he was free and staggered up, blindly and dizzily, ready to renew the strife. He halted, frozen. Down the slope the vampire horde was fleeing and over their heads and close at their shoulders flew huge vultures, tearing and rending avidly, sinking their beaks in the dead flesh, devouring the creatures as they fled.

Kane laughed, almost insanely.

"Defy man and God, but you may not deceive the vultures, sons of Satan! They know whether a man be alive or dead!"

N'Longa stood like a prophet on the pinnacle, and the great blackbirds soared and wheeled about him. His arms still waved and his voice still wailed out across the hills. And over the skylines they came, hordes on endless hordes—vultures, vultures, vultures! come to the feast so long denied them. They blackened the sky with their numbers, blotted out the sun; a strange darkness fell on the land. They settled in long dusky lines, diving into the caverns with a whir of wings and a clash of beaks. Their talons tore at the evil horrors which these caves disgorged.

Now all the vampires were fleeing to their city. The vengeance held back for ages had come down on them and their last hope was the heavy walls which had kept back the desperate human foes. Under those crumbling roofs they might find shelter. And N'Longa watched them stream into the city, and he laughed until the crags re-echoed.

Now all were in and the birds settled like a cloud over the doomed city, perching in solid rows along the walls, sharpening their beaks and claws on the towers.

And N'Longa struck flint and steel to a bundle of dry leaves he had brought with him. The bundle leaped into instant flame and he straightened and flung the blazing thing far out over the cliffs. It fell like a meteor to the plateau beneath, showering sparks. The tall grass of the plateau leaped aflame.

From the silent city beneath them Fear flowed in unseen waves, like a white fog. Kane smiled grimly.

"The grass is sere and brittle from the drouth." he said; "there has been even less rain than usual this season; it will burn swiftly."

Like a crimson serpent the fire ran through the high dead grass. It spread and it spread and Kane, standing high above, yet felt the fearful intensity of the hundreds of red eyes which watched from the stone city.

Now the scarlet snake had reached the walls and was rearing as if to coil and writhe over them. The vultures rose on heavily flapping wings and soared reluctantly. A vagrant gust of wind whipped the blaze about and drove it in a long red sheet around the wall. Now the city was hemmed in on all sides by a solid barricade of flame. The roar came up to the two men on the high crag.

Sparks flew across the wall, lighting in the high grass in the streets. A score of flames leaped up and grew with terrifying speed. A veil of red cloaked streets and buildings, and through this crimson, whirling mist Kane and N'Longa saw hundreds of dark shapes scamper and writhe, to vanish suddenly in red bursts of flame. There rose an intolerable scent of decayed flesh burning.

Kane gazed, awed. This was truly a hell on earth. As in a nightmare he looked into the roaring red cauldron where dark insects fought against their doom and perished. The flames leaped a hundred feet into the air, and suddenly above their roar sounded one bestial, inhuman scream like a shriek from across nameless gulfs of cosmic space, as one vampire, dying, broke the chains of silence which had held him for untold centuries. High and haunting it rose, the death cry of a vanishing race.

Then the flames dropped suddenly. The conflagration had been a typical grass fire, short and fierce. Now the plateau showed a blackened expanse and the city a charred and smoking mass of crumbling stone. Not one corpse lay in view, not even a charred bone. Above all whirled the dark swarms of the vultures, but they, too, were beginning to scatter.

Kane gazed hungrily at the clean blue sky. Like a strong sea wind clearing a fog of horror was the sight to him. From somewhere sounded the faint and far-off roaring of a distant lion. The vultures were flapping away in black, straggling lines.

CHAPTER 5

PALAVER SET!

Kane sat in the mouth of the cave where Zunna lay, submitting to the fetish-man's bandaging.

The Puritan's garments hung in tatters about his frame; his limbs and breast were deeply gashed and darkly bruised, but he had had no mortal wound in that deathly fight on the cliff.

"Mighty men, we be!" declared N'Longa with deep approval. "Vampire city be silent now, sure 'nough! No walking dead man live along these hills."

"I do not understand," said Kane, resting chin on hand. "Tell me, N'Longa, how have you done things?

How talked you with me in my dreams; how came you into the body of Kran; and how summoned you the vultures?"

"My blood-brother," said N'Longa, discarding his pride in his pidgin English, to drop into the river language understood by Kane, "I am so old that you would call me a liar if I told you my age. All my life I have worked magic, sitting first at the feet of mighty ju-ju men of the south and the east; then I was a slave to the Buckra and learned more. My brother, shall I span all these years in a moment and make you understand with a word, what has taken me so long to learn? I could not even make you understand how these vampires have kept their bodies from decay by drinking the lives of men.

"I sleep and my spirit goes out over the jungle and the rivers to talk with the sleeping spirits of my friends. There is a mighty magic on the voodoo staff I gave you—a magic out of the Old Land which draws my ghost to it as a white man's magic draws metal."

Kane listened unspeaking, seeing for the first time in N'Longa's glittering eyes something stronger and deeper than the avid gleam of the worker in black magic. To Kane it seemed almost as if he looked into the far-seeing and mystic eyes of a prophet of old.

"I spoke to you in dreams," N'Longa went on, and I made a deep sleep come over the souls of Kran and Zunna, and remove them to a far dim land, whence they shall soon return, unremembering. All things bow to magic, blood-brother, and beasts and birds obey the master words. I worked strong voodoo, vulture-magic, and the flying people of the air gathered at my call.

"These things I know and am a part of, but how shall I tell you of them? Blood-brother, you are a mighty warrior, but in the ways of magic you are as a little child lost. And what has taken me long dark years to know, I may not divulge to you so you would understand. My friend, you think only of bad spirits, but were my magic always bad, should I not take this fine young body in place of my old wrinkled one and keep it? But Kran shall have his body back safely.

"Keep the voodoo staff, blood-brother. It has mighty power against all sorcerers and serpents and evil things. Now I return to the village on the Coast where my true body sleeps. And what of you, my blood-brother?"

Kane pointed silently eastward.

"The call grows no weaker. I go."

N'Longa nodded, held out his hand. Kane grasped it. The mystical expression had gone from the fetish-man's face and the eyes twinkled snakily with a sort of reptilian mirth.

"Me go now, blood-brother," said the fetish-man, returning to his beloved jargon, of which knowledge he was prouder than all his conjuring tricks. "You take care—that one fellow jungle, she pluck your bones yet! Remember that voodoo stave, brother. Ai ya, palaver set!"

He fell back on the sand, and Kane saw the keen, sly expression of N'Longa fading from the face of Kran. His flesh crawled again. Somewhere back on the Slave Coast, the body of N'Longa, withered and wrinkled, was stirring in the ju-ju hut, was rising as if from a deep sleep. Kane shuddered.

Kran sat up, yawned, stretched and smiled. Beside him the girl Zunna rose, rubbing her eyes.

"Master," said Kran apologetically, "we must have slumbered."

HAWK OF BASTI*

"Solomon Kane!"

The interlapping branches of the great trees rose in mighty arches, hundreds of feet above the moss-carpeted earth, making a Gothic twilight among the giant trunks. Was this witchcraft? Who, in this heathen, forgotten land of shadowy mysteries, broke the brooding silence to shout the name of a strange wanderer?

Kane's cold eyes roved among the trees; one lean iron hand hardened on the carved, sharp-pointed stave he carried, the other hovered near one of the long flintlock pistols he wore.

Then from among the shadows stepped a bizarre figure. Kane's eyes widened slightly. A white man it was, strangely clad. A silken loincloth was his only garment, and he wore curious sandals on his feet. Armlets of gold and a heavy golden chain about his neck increased the barbarity of his appearance, as well as the hoop-like rings in his ears. But while the other ornaments were of curious and unfamiliar workmanship, the earrings were such as Kane had seen hundreds of times in the ears of European seamen.

The man was scratched and bruised as if he had been racing through thick woods recklessly; there were shallow gashes on his limbs and body that no thorn or bramble could have made. In his right hand he held a short curved sword, dyed a sinister red.

"Solomon Kane, by the howling hounds of hell!" exclaimed this man, glaring in amazement as he ap-

---
* Completed by J. Ramsey Campbell.

proached the staring Englishman. "Keelhaul me from Satan's craft, but you gave me a start! I thought to be the only white man for a thousand miles!"

"I had thought the same of myself," answered Kane. "But I know you not."

The other laughed harshly.

"I wonder not thereat," quoth he. "Belike I'd scarce know myself should I meet myself suddenly. Well, Solomon, my sober cutthroat, it's been many a year since I gazed on that sombre face of yours, but I'd know it in Hades. Come, have you forgotten the brave old days when we harried the Dons from the Azores to Darien and back again? Cutlass and carronade! By the bones of the saints, ours was a red trade! You've not forgotten Jeremy Hawk!"

Recognition glimmered in Kane's cold eyes as a shadow passes across the surface of a frozen lake.

"I remember; we did not sail on the same ship, though. I was with Sir Richard Grenville. You sailed with John Bellefonte."

"Aye!" cried Hawk with an oath. "I'd give the crown I've lost to live those days again! But Sir Richard's at the bottom of the sea, and Bellefonte's in hell, and many of the bold brethren are swinging in chains or feeding the fishes with good English flesh. Tell me, my melancholy murderer, does good Queen Bess still rule old England?"

"It's been many moons since I left our native shores," answered Kane. "She sat firmly on her throne when I sailed."

He spoke shortly, and Hawk stared at him curiously. "You never loved the Tudors, eh, Solomon?"

"Her sister harried my people like beasts of prey," answered Kane harshly. "She herself has lied to and betrayed the folk of my faith—but that's neither here nor there. What do you here?"

Hawk, Kane noticed, from time to time turned his head and stared back in the direction from which he had come, in an attitude of close listening, as if he expected pursuit.

"It's a long story," he answered. "I'll tell it briefly—you know there were high words between Bellefonte and others of the English captains—"

"I've heard he became no better than a common pirate," Kane said bluntly.

Hawk grinned wickedly. "Why, so they said. At any rate, away to the Main we sailed, and by Satan's eyes, we lived like kings among the isles, preying on the plate ships and treasure galleons. Then came a Spanish warship and harried us sore. A bursting cannon shot sent Bellefonte to his master, the Devil, and I, as first mate, became captain. There was a French rogue name La Costa who opposed me—well, I hanged La Costa to the main-yards and squared sails for the south. We gave the warship the slip at last, and made for the Slave Coast for a cargo of black ivory. But our luck went with Bellefonte. We piled on a reef in a heavy fog and when the mist cleared, a hundred war-canoes full of naked, howling devils were swarming about us.

"We fought for half a day, and when we had beaten them off, we found ourselves nearly out of powder, half our men dead, and the ship ready to slip off the reef where she hung and sink under our feet. There were but two things to do: take to sea in open boats or come ashore. And there was but one boat the bombards of the warship had left unshattered. Some of the crew piled into it, and the last we saw of them, they were rowing westward. The rest of us got ashore on rafts.

"By the gods of Hades! It was madness—but what else was there for us to do? The jungles swarmed with blood-lusting savages. We marched northward, hoping to come upon a barracoon where slavers came, but they cut us off, and we turned due eastward perforce. We fought every step of the way; our band melted like mist before the sun. Spears and savage beasts and venomous serpents took their fearful toll. At last I alone faced the jungle that had swallowed all my men. I eluded the natives. For months I travelled alone and all but unarmed in this hostile land. At last I came out upon the shores of a great lake and saw the walls and towers of an island kingdom rising before me."

Hawk laughed fiercely. "By the bones of the saints! It sounds like a tale of Sir John Mandeville! I found a strange people upon the islands—and a curious and ungodly race who ruled over them. They had never seen a white man before. In my youth I wandered about with a band of thieves who masked their real characters by tumbling and juggling. By virtue of my skill at sleight o'hand, I impressed the people. They looked on me as a god—all except old Agara, their priest—and he could not explain away my white skin.

"They made a fetish of me and old Agara secretly offered to make me a high priest. I appeared to acquiesce and learned many of his secrets. I feared the old vulture at first, for he could make magic that made my sleight o'hand seem childish—but the people were strongly drawn to me.

"The lake is called Nyayna; the isles thereon are named the Isles of Ra, and the main island is called Basti. The ruling class called themselves Khabasti and the slaves are named Masutos.

"The life of the latter is wretched indeed. They have no will of their own save the desires of their cruel masters. They are more brutally treated than the Indians of Darien are treated by the Spanish. I have seen women flogged to death and men crucified for the slightest of faults. The cult of Khabasti is a dark and bloody one, which they brought with them from whatever foul land they came from. On the great altar in the temple of the Moon, each week a howling victim dies beneath old Agara's dagger—always a Masuto sacrifice, a strong young lad or a virgin. Nor is that the worst—before the dagger brings relief from suffering, the victim is mutilated in ways hideous to mention. The Holy Inquisition pales before the tortures inflicted by Basti's priests; yet so hellish is their art that the gibbering, mowing, blind and skinless creature lives until the final thrust of the dagger speeds him or her beyond the reach of the torturing devils."

Hawk's covert glance showed him that deep volcanic fires were beginning to smolder coldly in Kane's strange eyes. His expression became more darkly brooding than ever, as he motioned the buccaneer to continue.

"No Englishman could look on the daily agonies of the poor wretches without pity. I became their champion as soon as I learned the language, and I took the part of the Masutos. Then old Agara would have slain me, but the slaves rose and slew the fiend who held the throne. Then they begged me to remain and rule them. I did so. Under my rule Basti prospered, both the Masutos and the Khabasti. But old Agara, who had slunk away to some secret hiding place, was working in the shadows. He plotted against me and finally even turned many of the Masutos against their deliverer. The poor fools! Yesterday he came out in the open and in a pitched battle, the streets of ancient Basti ran red. But old Agara prevailed with his evil magic, and most of my adherents were cut down. We retreated in canoes to one of the lesser islands, and there they came upon us, and again we lost the fight. All of my henchmen were slain or taken—and God help those taken alive!—only I escaped. They have hunted me like wolves since. Even now they are hard on my track. They will not rest until they slay me, if they have to first follow me across the continent."

"Then we should waste no time in talk," said Kane, but Hawk smiled coldly.

"Nay—the moment I glimpsed you through the trees and realized that by some strange whim of Fate I had met a man of my own race, I saw that again I should wear the golden, gem-set circlet that is the crown of Basti. Let them come—we will go and meet them!

"Harkee, my bold Puritan, what I did before, I did unarmed, by sheer craft o'head. Had I a firearm, I had been ruler in Basti at this hour. They never heard of powder. You have two pistols—enough to make us kings a dozen times over—but would you had a musket."

Kane shrugged his shoulders. Needless to tell Hawk of the fiendish battle in which his musket had been splintered; even now he wondered if that ghastly episode had not been a vision of delirium.

"I have weapons enow," said he, "though my supply of powder and shot be limited."

"Three shots will put us on the throne of Basti," quoth Hawk. "How, my brave broadbrim, wilt chance it with an old comrade?"

"I will aid you in all that it be my power," answered Kane sombrely. "But I wish no earthly throne of pride and vanity. If we bring peace to a suffering race and punish evil men for their cruelty, it is enough for me."

They made a strange contrast, those two, standing there in the twilight of that great tropic forest. Jeremy Hawk was as tall as Solomon Kane and like him was rangy and powerful—steel springs and whalebone. But where Solomon was dark, Jeremy Hawk was blond. Now he was burned to light bronze by the sun, and his tangled yellow locks fell over his high narrow forehead. His jaw, masked by a yellow stubble, was lean and aggressive; his thin gash of a mouth was cruel. His gray eyes were gleaming and restless, full of wild glitterings and shifting lights. His nose was thin and aquiline, and his whole face was that of a bird of prey. He stood, leaning slightly forward in his usual attitude of fierce eagerness, nearly naked, gripping his reddened sword.

Facing him stood Solomon Kane, likewise tall and powerful, in his worn boots, tattered garments, and featherless slouch hat, girt with pistols, rapier, and dagger; with his powder-and-shot pouch slung to his belt. There was no hint of likeness between the wild, reckless hawk's face of the buccaneer and the sombre features of the Puritan, whose dark pallor rendered his face almost corpse-like. Yet in the tigerish litheness of the pirate, in the wolfish appearance of Kane the same quality was apparent. Both of these men were born rovers and killers, curst with a paranoid driving urge that burned them like a quenchless fire and never gave them rest.

"Give me one of your pistols," exclaimed Hawk, "and half your powder and shot. They will soon be upon us—by Judas, we won't await them! We'll go to meet them! Leave it all to me—one shot and they will fall down and worship us. Come! And as we go, tell me how you come to be here."

"I have wandered for many moons," said Kane, half-reluctantly. "Why I am here I know not—but the jungle called me across many leagues of blue sea, and I came. Doubtless the same Providence which hath guided my steps all my years has led me hither for some purpose which my weak eyes have not yet seen."

"You carry a strange stick," said Hawk, as they moved with long, swinging strides beneath the huge arches.

Kane's eyes drifted to the stave in his right hand. It was as long as a sword, hard as iron, and sharpened at the smaller end. The other end was carved in the shape of a cat's head, and all up and down the stave were strange wavering lines and curious carvings.

"I doubt not but that it is a thing of black magic and sorcery," said Kane sombrely. "But in time past it hath prevailed mightily against beings of darkness, and it is a goodly weapon. It was given me by a strange creature—one N'Longa, a fetish man of the Slave Coast, whom I have seen perform nameless and ungodly feats. Yet beneath his savage and wrinkled hide beats the heart of a true man, I doubt not."

"Hark!" Hawk halted, stiffening suddenly. From ahead of them sounded the tramp of many sandaled feet—faint as a wind in the tree-tops, yet, keen-eared as hunting hounds, both he and his companion heard and translated it.

"There's a glade just ahead," grinned Hawk fiercely. "We'll await them there—"

And so Kane and the ex-king of Basti stood in plain view at one side of the glade when a hundred men burst from the other side, like a pack of wolves on a hot trail. They stopped in amazement, struck speechless at the sight of he who had been fleeing for his life and who now faced them with a cruel, mocking smile —and at the sight of his silent companion.

As for Kane, he gazed at them in wonder. Half of them were negroes, stocky, burly fellows, with barrel chests and short legs of men who spend much of their time in canoes. They were naked and armed with heavy spears. It was the others who arrested the Englishman's attention. These were tall, well-formed men whose regular features and straight black hair showed scant trace of negroid blood. Their color was a coppery brown, ranging from a light reddish tan to a deep bronze. Their faces were open and not unpleasing. Their garments consisted only of sandals and silken loincloths. On their heads many wore a sort of helmet made of bronze, and each bore on his left arm a small round buckler of wood, reinforced with hardened hide and braced with copper nails. Their arms were curved swords similar to that borne by Hawk, polished wooden maces, and light battle-axes. Some carried heavy bows of evident power and quivers of long barbed arrows.

And it came forcibly to Solomon Kane that somewhere he had seen men much like these, or pictures of men like them. But where he could not say. They halted in the midst of the glade, to gaze uncertainly at the two white men.

"Well," said Hawk, mockingly, "you have found your king—have you forgotten your duty to your ruler? Down on your knees, dogs!"

A well-built young warrior at the head of the men spoke passionately, and Kane started as he realized that he understood the language. It was much akin to the numerous Bantu dialects, many of which Kane had picked up in his travels, though some of the words were unintelligible to him and had a tang of peculiar antiquity.

"Red-handed murderer!" exclaimed the youth, his dark cheeks flushing in anger. "You dare to mock us? I know not who this man is, but our quarrel is not with him; it is your head that we will take back to Agara with us. Seize him—"

His own hand went back with the javelin he carried, and in that instant Hawk aimed deliberately and fired. The heavy-bored pistol crashed deafeningly, and in the smoke Kane saw the young warrior drop like a dog. The effect on the rest was just as Kane had seen it be on savages in many other lands. Their weapons slipped from nerveless hands, and they stood frozen, gaping like frightened children. Some of the warriors cried out and dropped to their knees or flat on their faces.

The distended eyes of all were drawn as by a magnet to the silent corpse. At the close range, the heavy ball had literally shattered the youth's skull—had blasted out his brains. And while his comrades stood like sheep, Hawk struck while the iron was hot.

"Down, dogs!" he cried sharply, striding forward and striking a warrior to his knees with a blow of his open hand. "Shall I loose the thunders of death upon you all, or will you receive me again as your rightful king?"

Dazed, brains numbed, the warriors sank to their knees; some wriggled prostrate on their bellies and whimpered. Hawk placed his heel on the neck of the nearest warrior and grinned savagely and triumphantly at Kane.

"Arise," said he, with a contemptuous kick. "But none forget I am king! Will ye return to Basti and fight for me, or will ye all die here?"

"We will fight for you, master," came the answering chorus. Hawk grinned again.

"Retaking the throne is easier than even I thought," said he. "Rise now—leave that carrion where it has fallen. I am your king, and this is Solomon Kane, my comrade. He is a terrible magician, and even if you should slay me—who am immortal—he will blast you all out of existence."

Men are sheep, thought Solomon, as he saw the warriors of both factions meekly forming themselves according to Hawk's orders. They formed short ranks, three abreast, and in the center walked Kane and Hawk.

"No fear of a spear in the back," said the buccaneer to Kane. "They are cowed—see the dazed look in their eyes? Yet be on guard."

Then calling to a man who had the appearance of a chief, he ordered him to walk between himself and Kane.

"Tell me of Agara," he bade the man. "Does he celebrate his brief victory?"

"No, master." Though he was as tall as they, the man could not conceal his wariness of the two pale men. Perhaps their color seemed as magical to him as the pistol-shot. "He had the bodies of the slain taken to the fields, to help the next sowing," the man muttered. "Now he prepares the temple of the Moon. Tonight the Moon reveals her whole face," he whispered, uneasily averting his eyes from the sky.

"He'll offer up a sacrifice to thank her for his victory, will he? Aye, the moon will have her sacrifice," Hawk growled; a thin smile glinted like a curved blade amid his stubble. "But it won't be the victim the priest intends."

He gestured the chief to rejoin the ranks of warriors, and laughed aloud at the stumbling haste of the man. "By Satan's blood," he said to Kane in English, "we'll show these dogs what it means to be ruled by an English king!"

Kane frowned, and glanced back. Might not Hawk be over-estimating his power? The stocky spear-men looked nervous; the pistol had done its work well. But the taller men, three of whom strode at the rear, while the rest preceded Kane and Hawk—their eyes gleamed sullenly, dull embers that might grow to anger. Perhaps it was only the light of the lowering sun, which glared between the immense trees like a Cyclopean eye engorged with blood.

Hawk had taken his frown for disapproval. "By God's wounds!" he cried. "What's this, an Englishman with no spirit for conquest? Time's robbed you of your manhood, my old prayer-teller, since I saw you paint your cutlass bright red in men's guts!"

Kane's hand twitched toward his rapier. But he knew the extravagances of Hawk's speech. "Think ye I would hesitate to do battle with evil?" he demanded. "But mayhap you take these men's beliefs too lightly, to expect them to take arms against their god."

"Our pistols are stronger than gods." As Kane shook his head sombrely, Hawk went on "I am old in battle as you. Harkee, I have my strategy. The heathen cower in their rooms in terror of moonrise, and their priest skulks in his temple. And our men have no thought of deposing their god, but only of seating their rightful king on his throne again."

Kane's long easy stride concealed his unease. But he could scarcely leave his fellow countryman alone amid the warriors. He could only trust Providence, yet he felt rather at its mercy. Still, he had no doubt that there was evil to be quashed in Basti.

The sun's disc had subsided. Its red glow dimmed, deep in the jungle. The trees and undergrowth turned ashen with twilight, as though a fire had died. Distant lions sounded like the awakening of a storm; closer, the jungle threshed and rustled—the night's predators were abroad. Between the trees Kane glimpsed far peaks, whitened by the rising moon. They looked cruel as stone knives.

Except that the ground was growing softer underfoot, Kane had no warning of the nearness of the lake until the trees abruptly thinned and at once gave out entirely. The water was wide and still, and seemed unnaturally silent. Kane made out several dark forms, huge and dormant, far across the lake. They must be islands, yet they made him think of somnolent monsters, dim and primeval. Thin blades of moonlight gleamed on the water.

The margin was overgrown by grass, strong and keen-edged. The chief whom Hawk had interrogated led the way, tramping firmly. Once a spear-man missed his footing, and Kane heard the ground suck the man's foot, eager as a vampire. Had their guide intended to trick them, Kane admitted grudgingly that he could have done so here. But Kane glanced warily at the moon's skull as it peered over the mountains.

Concealed by grass at the water's edge, two long canoes lay waiting. Kane boarded one, while Hawk climbed into the other. Each sat as far back as possible, to watch for treachery.

The stocky men rowed the canoes across the lake. The oars wallowed; the water sounded slow and thick as blood. The moon was clear of the mountains, and was scattered broken on the lake. Kane had seen men maddened by its light; worse, he had seen creatures that seemed human grow pelt and claws and fangs. How much greater might be the power of that light over these men, to whom the moon was the manifestation of their god?

As the light blazed coldly in the clear sky, he saw what was carved on the prow. At first he had thought it was a swollen flower. It was an image of the moon, surrounded by rays that curved inward like claws. Was it convex or concave? An orb, or a mouth? It made him flex his shoulders angrily. In the nearby craft, Hawk watched grimly over his crew.

A dark bulk rose against the moon: an enormous crown, or a head with several horns? It was the largest island, brandishing a group of silent pyramids. The hushed rowers ferried him across black water sown by moonlight; the tall coppery men gazed at the moon. He felt as if he had been tricked into participating in a ritual, ancient and evil. He gripped the cat-headed voodoo stave, which had once saved him from an occult danger: N'Longa, the voodoo man, had sent his spirit to inhabit the body of Kane's companion, so that he might have an experienced ally.

The craft reached a deserted wharf. Other canoes, and larger boats, nodded in the moonlight. Now Kane could see that the pyramids were surrounded by a massive wall. This, then, was the city of Basti.

Fields of grain gleamed white beneath the moon. Between them, a wide tramped path led to the city. The men formed ranks and began to advance. Kane sensed their growing reluctance. The moon's face blazed amid the pyramids, like the mask of a god in a temple.

Hawk moved alongside Kane. Plots brooded in his eyes. "Harkee, Kane," he muttered. "What say you to converting these heathen swine to your god? That'd be a fine feather for a Puritan's cap, eh?"

Kane shook his head. Hawk's ruse failed to tempt him. He would tarry only long enough to quash the cruelty of Agara the priest. Hawk seemed in the grip of ambition—too convinced of his own power to plan strategies. What if ambush awaited them at the city?

He was about to put that question when the buccaneer glared at the men. Now they were near the looming walls their pace was slackening. "March on, you dogs," Hawk growled. "We'll enter my city like a king and his men, not like a creeping priest."

But they had halted, yards short of the wall. The sky was steeped in the dead glow of the moon. Kane made out gates so colossal that the two helmeted guards who stood beside them seemed dwarfs. The gates were framed by dozens of clawed moons.

Perhaps Hawk saw the guards as mere dwarfs. He strode forward, snarling, "Open the gates to your king!"

The men did not speak, and hardly moved. Only when Hawk was almost at the gates did they raise their curved swords in silent warning. Their action seemed ritualistic; their task must be to keep the city inviolate while the rites of the moon were performed.

Hawk scarcely glanced at them. He flourished the pistol at them, growling an oath, then raised the weapon to hammer on the gates. Moving like reflections of each other, the guards closed on him with the unearthly grace of moonlit waves, blades ready to split him open before and behind.

Kane shouted warning. But Hawk was not so unaware as he had seemed. He ducked aside, quick as a lizard, and discharged his pistol at the face of the older guard. The man was hurled against the gates; the right side of his head, now earless, glittered blackly in the moonlight.

The younger guard recovered his footing and rushed at Hawk, blade ready to spill his entrails. For a moment he stared at the pistol, trembling; then he read in Hawk's glance that it was spent, for he grinned with wild bravado. Hawk dodged, but the blade almost opened his belly. Kane ran toward them. He could not yet be sure of a clear shot at the youth.

Suddenly Hawk tripped on a hummock and fell, trapping his undrawn sword beneath him. The curved blade sliced down to mutilate him. His heels dug into the ground and thrust him sliding, so that the sword impaled the ground between his legs. Before the youth could pluck out the blade, Hawk clubbed him across the face with the pistol, shattering his jaw. He curled up, moaning.

As Hawk rose, the older guard shoved himself away from the gate and lurched toward him, brandishing his sword and spiked mace. Blood, blackened by the moonlight, gushed down his cheek. Hawk seemed obsessed with the pistol, for he had forgotten that he had a sword; he retreated, struggling to reload. But the guard was upon him too quickly, raising his weapons so that Kane could hardly see his face. Kane's shot exploded the guard's chest.

The guard staggered back. Then, although the ragged wound in his chest poured blood down his torso, he advanced doggedly. Hearing Kane's shot, and seeing its effect, the kneeling buccaneer had taken his time in reloading; now, faced with the apparently indestructible guard, he was still fumbling.

Perhaps it was only fanaticism, but the sole life that Kane could distinguish in the guard's eyes was the flat cold shine of the moon. There was no time to reload. Drawing his dagger, Kane rushed at the guard from the side. Before the man could turn on him, ponderous as a zombie, Kane disembowelled him. The guard sank to his knees as his gaping belly vomited his innards on the earth. Even then the white light glowed in his eyes like a marsh-phantom, until Kane plunged the dagger into his heart.

Shuddering, Kane wiped his blade on the grass. Hawk clapped him on the shoulder. "Aye, old comrade," he cried, "you've lost none of your taste for the bloody trade."

He seemed not at all disconcerted, to Kane's dismay. "Now let's to the throne of Basti!" the buccaneer shouted. "By Satan's wings, I'll be in my rightful place before the moon sets!"

Stalking to the gates, he drummed on them with his pistol until they resounded. The ranks of men waited uneasily, as did Kane. Why was the city so silent, when the shots must have echoed through the streets? Were the people intent on their ritual, or lying in wait?

Without warning, the gates began to groan. Creaking, they drew back, gradually and solemnly. It was as though a mountain had parted to reveal secret pyramids, piebald with moonlight and shadow. Within the gates ranks of silent people stood, tall ones and stocky, perhaps two hundred of them. Moonlight spilled out of the city like a waterfall, and silhouetted a lone robed figure, tall and very thin.

The man moved forward; the light caught his face. It was thin as a skull. Though it bore a kind of dignity, that dignity seemed withered or gone bad. The man's robes were embroidered with rayed moons, which swarmed on him like spiders. Was there a vicious glint in his eyes, or a reflection of the moon? At once it was gone, ousted by a look of resignation.

Kane did not need Hawk's growl of anger to tell him that this was the priest, Agara. Hawk levelled his pistol at Agara's face. But the priest spread his arms wide in a gesture of submissive welcome; his long translucent fingernails gleamed. He bowed low to Hawk and then, with what seemed a faint smile of pleased surprise, to Kane. "Basti welcomes the chosen of the moon," he said, in a voice dead and cold as that orb.

At once all the silent people within the gates prostrated themselves, touching the ground with their foreheads. "By Satan's bowels, Kane," Hawk whispered, "the old savage knows he's beaten."

Kane was wary. "Is he their sole priest?" he demanded.

"Aye. And may Jeremy Hawk be flayed alive by devils if there's ever another," the buccaneer vowed grimly.

Still Kane was wary. Perhaps Agara had realized that his time was coming to an end, and had decided to yield rather than be beaten ignominiously. But in Kane's experience that was not the way of priests.

However, Hawk seemed overwhelmed by the welcome. As the ranks of citizens rose to their feet, heads bowed, he gestured his warriors and Kane to accompany him, then strode into the city as though it were his home.

Outside the gates the young guard still lay clenched and moaning. "See that he is taken care of," Hawk commanded the priest magnanimously. Kane thought he was trying to sound like a king.

The buccaneer gestured his men to form ranks more precisely. "Aye, that's the style for a king's men," he said to Kane, then to the warriors, "Now you'll escort me to my throne."

"No!" Agara cried. It sounded like a plea. "It must be done as our god decrees. Tomorrow," he shouted to the silent citizens, "the city of Basti welcomes the pale men to their appointed place."

If Hawk agreed to the priest's demands it might reinforce Agara's power. But the priest was alone, and to be enthroned as tradition decreed would surely strengthen Hawk's kingship. "Very well," the buccaneer said. "As your king, I will uphold tradition."

Agara led the Englishmen and the warriors through the wide streets. Against the moon, the pyramids seemed massive and inhuman as mountains; Kane felt he was walking through a dead city. No doubt the battle between Hawk and Agara had reduced the population cruelly. At the centre of the city, on the highest pyramid, hundreds of steps climbed to a circular moonlit temple.

Bearing torches, they climbed the narrow ramped passages within the second highest pyramid, leaving warriors at each level. The topmost cell was spacious. Hammocks were strung in the corners; trestle tables bore elaborately worked pottery. Embroidered hangings depicted battles and heroic deeds, every one watched over by an embroidered moon. Kane strode onto the stone balcony, to assure himself that it could not be reached easily from below. Beneath the low moon he saw Agara, drifting toward his temple like a shadow.

"Satan's bones, Kane," Hawk complained, "a king shouldn't have to climb so far to bed!"

They took turns to keep watch. Hawk vowed he would be easy in his mind once he was enthroned. In his sleep Kane dreamed that N'Longo, the voodoo man, visited him. The wizened black face seemed to swim in fog, and was impossible for Kane to focus. But he knew the old droning voice, and the old man's pidgin English, his most prized possession. "You not be fraid give one fellow voodoo staff to Hawk," N'Longa said.

Before he could question N'Longa's meaning, an atrocious scream woke Kane. It was the cry of a man in incredible agony. Kane leaped from his hammock, pistol ready in his hand. He followed Hawk onto the balcony. But the streets were silent; only the echoes of agony throbbed in Kane's ears.

Had the wretch ceased suffering? Kane suspected he had only been prevented from uttering any further sound. Hawk glared red-eyed at the deserted streets. "If that's more of Agara's torture I'll flay him myself," he said with an oath.

The exhaustion of the previous day's flight dulled his fury. Kane let him sleep, and watched dawn spread like a slow raw wound above the jungle and the mountains, staining the lake. Hours later the buccaneer woke, roaring "By the saints, I'll be keelhauled if I don't know who screamed. It was the guard I told that savage to nurse."

He stormed out of the building. Kane followed him down the dim ramps, but was wary enough to carry a torch. Hawk strode up the wide steps toward the temple. Halfway up he halted, purple-faced with anger, and roared "Agara!"

Eventually the priest emerged. In the daylight he looked ashen, as though bone were showing through his skin, and unhealthy as a creature unused to the sun. "Where is the guard I entrusted to you?" Hawk demanded.

"He died of his wound in the night," the lifeless voice said gently. "He choked to death on his own blood."

Disarmed, Hawk nonetheless shouted, "Show me his corpse!"

The voice drifted down, cold as moonlight. "He has already been given to the earth."

"And who screamed in the night, you damned heathen?"

"That was the guard, as he died. The pain of his injury was so great."

The priest withdrew. Glowering, Hawk beckoned Kane to join him. "By the entrails of all the saints, I'll not be refused so!" he roared, and tramped up the steps to the temple.

Kane anticipated trouble, and had his pistol ready. But the priest was alone, and watched their search with a flickering smile. There was no sign of the guard's body. The circular temple was little more than a high wall, open to the sky, containing several altars from which ran grooves. Everywhere the moon was carved, as though the stone were covered with boils.

"Then we'll search the city," Hawk sneered at Agara, and strode to wake his men.

Though he was obscurely troubled by the waste of daylight, Kane accompanied him in the search. At least the sacrifice to the full moon was past; that was grimly reassuring. Many of the cells in the pyramids they searched were deserted—and even the inhabited rooms were almost bare, except for a few pieces of stark furniture. Like the religion, the city was dying.

"Who screamed in the night?" Hawk demanded incessantly, but nobody would speak. Kane saw that they had been hushed at the gates not in awe of Hawk, but in terror of Agara. In the hives of cells, every wall was carved with the moon. In places other motives had been erased. Clearly Agara's religion had been determined to establish itself.

Hawk searched outside the city. Eventually they found, leading into a field of grain, a track of fresh blood as wide as a man. It grew too faint to trace its ending. Hawk trudged back to the city, his frown growing blacker as the twilight did. "No dried-up old savage disobeys Hawk of Basti," he muttered, and Kane realized that it was not the guard's suffering that troubled him.

Though the gates were open, the streets were deserted. Only the pyramids loomed within the walls. Amid the silence and the dying twilight they seemed even more like massive tombs. Kane and Hawk paced warily into the city, followed by the warriors. Hawk glared as arrows rattled faintly in the men's quivers.

"If this is one of the old heathen's tricks," he muttered, "I'll spill his guts down the steps of his temple."

Abruptly he gestured the men to halt. Ahead, beyond a pyramid, the twilight was flickering. He and Kane moved stealthily to a vantage-point.

In the street at the foot of the temple steps a dozen long trestle tables had been set up. The entire population of Basti sat there, as silent as though the tables were altars. One long table was vacant. Nearest the steps sat Agara, alone. Next to him, two elaborately carved wooden seats were empty. Before him on the table a crown glowed and glittered.

The priest rose. Surely he could not see the Englishmen—yet he gazed toward them as he cried, "At last those we honor have returned."

Angered, the buccaneer stalked sullenly to the place beside Agara. He sat glaring. Kane took his place beside him, while the warriors sat at the vacant table. They seemed cowed by the ritual feast, for they glanced uneasily at Agara as he cried, "Let the feast commence!"

His voice was high. Was he trying to sound gleeful in the face of Hawk's triumph? His eyes were dead as the moon. Kane trusted him as little as he would have trusted a vampire playing host at table.

But Hawk grew heartier as the women laid dishes of elaborately prepared food and jugs of rice wine before him. He quaffed a jug and called for another. He seemed unconcerned that the rice and spiced meats were carefully arranged to represent clawed moons.

Agara drank little, even when crying, "Let us drink to the pale men, saviors of Basti!" Kane imitated his abstinence secretly, and let most of the wine he appeared to drink flow back into his jug. Moonlight crept through the city, toward the temple steps.

The buccaneer roared for another jug, and ignored Kane's admonition. His natural caution, and wanderer's restlessness, were suffocated by ambition and wine. He gazed with blurred rough admiration at a serving-woman, returning with a new heaped dish. "Let Satan take my manhood if I don't have that wench tonight," he mumbled.

Kane felt weighed down by food. Was that part of Agara's strategy? "No more," he said, gesturing the woman away. The moonlight had reached this table now. "Methinks," he said in a tone of command to the priest, "that it is time to present the crown."

The moon seemed to engorge the priest's eyes with light. "You speak truth," he said grinning. With a cry that seemed to pierce Kane's eardrums, he leaped up and pointed.

Poised over the temple, as though balanced there, blazed the full moon. It was its second night. Before Kane could act, the serving-woman's knife had cut his belt. Seizing his weapons as they fell, she hurled them into the darkness beside the pyramid.

Agara had done the same to Hawk, and warriors had surrounded Hawk's men, bows drawn. The priest stepped beyond the buccaneer's reach; the moons on his swaying robe stirred. He seized the crown and with a movement that gave the appearance of inevitability, placed it on his own head.

"My people!" he cried. "The pale men have been sent by the Moon to save us! She has set her color on them as a sign! Their blood spilled in the sacrifice shall make Basti great again!"

A murmur, timid but approving, rose from the crowd. Glaring about desperately for a weapon, Kane saw the voodoo stave lying before him, just within arm's reach. He lunged forward—but Hawk grabbed the stave. For a moment they struggled. "Let go, you God-smitten fool," Hawk snarled. "Let me challenge him."

Kane remembered N'Longa's words in the dream. Reluctantly he yielded, and Hawk stumbled to his feet. "Let him be king who excels in magic!" he roared.

Had he been less drunk, he might not have issued so desperate a challenge. But the crowd dared to encourage him. Agara needed no persuasion. Smiling cruelly, he motioned Hawk to begin.

Hawk twirled the stave, and almost dropped it. His

shadow in the moonlight imitated his clumsiness perfectly. Could Kane dodge in the shadows while everyone was distracted, and retrieve a weapon? But the woman stood behind him, knife poised, in a position where he could not take her unawares.

Then he saw that Hawk's deftness was improving. In his hands the stave multiplied; it became three— two of which he threw away. Kane saw them sail through the air, but never heard them fall. Now the stave writhed snake-like, though Kane knew that it was hard as iron. It lay writhing at Hawk's feet, then leaped back into his hand. He seemed bemused by his own skill; perhaps N'Longa's voodoo had come to his aid through the stave.

The crowd was rapt. Hawk passed the stave through his body, as though the wood were a magical blade that clove him. The priest's face tightened like a fist. Suddenly he raised one hand as if clawing the moon from the sky, and shrieked a word.

Whatever the word meant, its power was awful. Its presence filled the city, lurking huge and dark behind the pyramids, peering from the depths of the minds of all who had heard. The crowd trembled as though at the mercy of an earthquake; Hawk faltered.

Agara's hand sank, and covered his face momentarily. Then, though it had seemed to contain something, it came away empty. It revealed a frightful thing. Agara's face had paled unnaturally; his eyes and all his features had grown vague. He had the face of the moon.

The crowd moaned, terrified. The priest turned toward them, his face glowing through the fabric of his hood. He seemed to snatch something from his face, and to cast it into their midst. At once the faces of the crowd were ousted. On the neck of everyone there the moon perched, a decayed grinning globe.

The moon within the hood turned. Its blotches of eyes gazed at Kane. Hawk brandished his stave; his teeth were chattering audibly. He stumbled toward the hooded figure, waving the stick as a powerless magician might wave his wand. The priest reached toward his glowing face again. The stave whirled trembling. Without warning Hawk thrust it, together with his whole weight, at the priest. Kane heard the point strike home.

The moon vanished from the hood. The priest's face appeared, screaming. He fell, and the stave pinned him to the earth. Though he was not slain, he was no longer a man.

"The pistols!" Hawk shouted to Kane.

The serving-woman was palsied with terror—as was the shivering crowd, whose faces were human again. Kane knocked the blade from her hand and darted into the shadows. Seizing the pistols, he reloaded them. He strode back and handed one to the buccaneer.

He expected Hawk to kill the writhing priest without further ado. But Hawk gazed at his victim with a gloating that contained little drunkenness. He had taken the crown, which sat rakishly on his tangled blond hair. "Now, my old pretender," he said softly, "we'll see how long it takes you to lose your skin."

Kane shot the priest, scattering his head over the blanched earth. Hawk turned snarling, and raised his pistol. His thin lips worked; his eyes gleamed, piercing as the gaze of the predator for which he was named.

Then one of the warriors who had done Agara's bidding approached hesitantly. Hawk whirled, and fired. The man's face exploded, crimsoning the air while the body flailed backward. "So perish all who do not swear allegiance now to Hawk of Basti!" the buccaneer roared, brandishing the voodoo stave like a scepter.

He was glaring at Kane. After all they had weathered, must they now duel? It seemed so, for the wild fury in the man's eyes looked determined to best Kane.

Suddenly those eyes flickered. Hawk's fingers opened, and wavered aimlessly as a baby's. His pistol fell unheeded. He began to strut about like a puppet of flesh. All at once he turned and grinned broadly at Kane.

Once before Kane had seen a man's face change thus. Still he could hardly believe. The eyes had steadied now, but they were not Hawk's eyes. Kane stared bewildered, until the thin mouth said "Ai ya— you not know N'Longa, blood-brother?"

Kane shook his head helplessly, too relieved to deplore the magic. "What have you done with Hawk?" he demanded.

"He go live along shadow-land. Maybe he learn be like king, he come back." He grinned, but his eyes were hard and ancient with experience. "This body go sit on king's throne, need king inside. Hawk no king. N'Longa better."

Kane could not sincerely disagree. The crowd watched, huddled together, confused and terrified. They needed a king. To call their hero by a new name would simply confuse them more. He raised the man's arm toward the glowing sky.

"Hail to the king," he shouted. "Hawk of Basti!"

As soon as it was daylight, Kane went to the wharf. People were already working in the fields; Hawk—or the man who had Hawk's body—was there, aiding and instructing them. He grinned widely as Kane hurried by.

Kane called men to a canoe, and had them row him to shore. His last glance backward at the island was uneasy. He felt that the city would always be haunted. Though it was full daylight now, above the jungle beyond the pyramids hovered the pale moon, like the ghost of the face that had peered from the hood.

THE RETURN OF
SIR RICHARD GRENVILLE

One slept beneath the branches dim,
    Cloaked in the crawling mist,
And Richard Grenville came to him
    And plucked him by the wrist.

No nightwind shook the forest deep
    Where the shadows of Doom were spread,
And Solomon Kane awoke from sleep
    And looked upon the dead.

He spake in wonder, not in fear:
    "How walks a man who died?
"Friend of old times, what do ye here,
    "Long fallen at my side?"

"Rise up, rise up," Sir Richard said,
    "The hounds of Doom are free;
"The slayers come to take your head
    "To hang on the ju-ju tree.

"Swift feet press the jungle mud
    "Where the shadows are grim and stark,
"And naked men who pant for blood
    "Are racing through the dark."

And Solomon rose and bared his sword,
    And swift as tongue could tell,
The dark spewed forth a painted horde
    Like shadows out of Hell.

His pistols thundered in the night,
    And in that burst of flame

He saw red eyes with hate alight,
  And on the figures came.

His sword was like a cobra's stroke
  And death hummed in its tune;
His arm was steel and knotted oak
  Beneath the rising moon.

But by him sang another sword,
  And a great form roared and thrust,
And dropped like leaves the screaming horde
  To writhe in bloody dust.

Silent as death their charge had been,
  Silent as night they fled;
And in the trampled glade was seen
  Only the torn dead.

And Solomon turned with outstretched hand,
  Then halted suddenly,
For no man stood with naked brand
  Beneath the moon-lit tree.

WINGS IN THE NIGHT

CHAPTER 1
THE HORROR ON THE STAKE

Solomon Kane leaned on his strangely carved staff and gazed in scowling perplexity at the mystery which spread silently before him. Many a deserted village Kane had seen in the months that had passed since he turned his face east from the Slave Coast and lost himself in the mazes of jungle and river, but never one like this.

It was not famine that had driven away the inhabitants, for yonder the wild rice still grew rank and unkempt in the untilled fields. There were no Arab slave-raiders in this nameless land—it must have been a tribal war that devastated the village, Kane decided, as he gazed sombrely at the scattered bones and grinning skulls that littered the space among the rank weeds and grasses. These bones were shattered and splintered, and Kane saw jackals and a hyena furtively slinking among the ruined huts. But why had the slayers left the spoils? There lay war spears, their shafts crumbling before the attacks of the white ants. There lay shields, moldering in the rains and sun. There lay the cooking pots, and about the neck-bones of a shattered skeleton glistened a necklace of gaudily painted pebbles and shells—surely rare loot for any savage conqueror.

He gazed at the huts, wondering why the thatch roofs of so many were torn and rent, as if by taloned things seeking entrance. Then something made his cold eyes narrow in startled unbelief. Just outside the moldering mound that was once the village wall towered a gigantic baobab tree, branchless for sixty feet, its mighty bole too large to be gripped and scaled. Yet in the topmost branches dangled a skeleton, apparently impaled on a broken limb.

The cold hand of mystery touched the shoulder of Solomon Kane. How came those pitiful remains in that tree? Had some monstrous ogre's inhuman hand flung them there?

Kane shrugged his broad shoulders and his hand unconsciously touched the black butts of his heavy pistols, the hilt of his long rapier, and the dirk in his belt. Kane felt no fear as an ordinary man would feel, confronted with the Unknown and Nameless. Years of wandering in strange lands and warring with strange creatures had melted away from brain, soul, and body all that was not steel and whalebone. He was tall and spare, almost gaunt, built with the savage economy of the wolf. Broad-shouldered, long-armed, with nerves of ice and thews of spring steel, he was no less the natural killer than the born swordsman.

The brambles and thorns of the jungle had dealt hardly with him; his garments hung in tatter, his featherless slouch hat was torn and his boots of Cordovan leather were scratched and worn. The sun had baked his chest and limbs to a deep bronze, but his ascetically lean face was impervious to its rays. His complexion was still of that strange, dark pallor which gave him an almost corpse-like appearance, belied only by his cold, light eyes.

And now Kane, sweeping the village once more with his searching gaze, pulled his belt into a more comfortable position, shifted to his left hand the cat-headed stave N'Longa had given him, and took up his way again.

To the west lay a strip of thin forest, sloping downward to a broad belt of savannas, a waving sea of grass waist-deep and deeper. Beyond that rose another narrow strip of woodlands, deepening rapidly into dense jungle. Out of that jungle Kane had fled like a hunted wolf with pointed-toothed men hot on his trail. Even now a vagrant breeze brought faintly the throb of a savage drum which whispered its obscene tale of hate and blood-hunger and belly-lust across miles of jungle and grassland.

The memory of his flight and narrow escape was vivid in Kane's mind, for only the day before had he realized too late that he was in cannibal country, and all that afternoon in the reeking stench of the thick jungle, he had crept and run and hidden and doubled and twisted on his track with the fierce hunters ever close behind him, until night fell and he gained and crossed the grasslands under cover of darkness.

Now in the late morning he had seen nothing, heard nothing of his pursuers, yet he had no reason to believe that they had abandoned the chase. They had been close on his heels when he took to the savannas.

So Kane surveyed the land in front of him. To the east, curving from north to south ran a straggling range of hills, for the most part dry and barren, rising in the south to a jagged black skyline that reminded Kane of the black hills of Negari. Between him and these hills stretched a broad expanse of gently rolling country, thickly treed, but nowhere approaching the density of a jungle. Kane got the impression of a vast upland plateau, bounded by the curving hills to the east and by the savannas to the west.

Kane set out for the hills with his long, swinging, tireless stride. Surely somewhere behind him the savage demons were stealing after him, and he had no desire to be driven to bay. A shot might send them flying in sudden terror, but on the other hand, so low they were in the scale of humanity, it might transmit no supernatural fear to their dull brains. And not even Solomon Kane, whom Sir Francis Drake had called Devon's king of swords, could win in a pitched battle with a whole tribe.

The silent village with its burden of death and mystery faded out behind him. Utter silence reigned among these mysterious uplands where no birds sang and only a silent macaw flitted among the great trees. The only sounds were Kane's cat-like tread, and the whisper of the drum-haunted breeze.

And then Kane caught a glimpse among the trees that made his heart leap with a sudden, nameless horror, and a few moments later he stood before Horror itself, stark and grisly. In a wide clearing, on a rather bold incline stood a grim stake, and to this stake was bound a thing that had once been a man. Kane had rowed, chained to the bench of a Turkish galley, and he had toiled in Barbary vineyards; he had battled red Indians in the New Lands and had languished in the dungeons of Spain's Inquisition. He knew much of the fiendishness of man's inhumanity, but now he shuddered and grew sick. Yet it was not so much the ghastliness of the mutilations, horrible as they were, that shook Kane's soul, but the knowledge that the wretch still lived.

For as he drew near, the gory head that lolled on the butchered breast lifted and tossed from side to side, spattering blood from the stumps of ears, while a bestial, rattling whimper drooled from the shredded lips.

Kane spoke to the ghastly thing and it screamed unbearably, writhing in incredible contortions, while its head jerked up and down with the jerking of mangled nerves, and the empty, gaping eye-sockets seemed striving to see from their emptiness. And moaning low and brain-shatteringly it huddled its outraged self against the stake where it was bound and lifted its head in a grisly attitude of listening, as if it expected something out of the skies.

"Listen," said Kane, in the dialect of the river tribes. "Do not fear me—I will not harm you and nothing else shall harm you any more. I am going to loose you."

Even as he spoke Kane was bitterly aware of the emptiness of his words. But his voice had filtered dimly into the rumbling, agony-shot brain of the man before him. From between splintered teeth fell words, faltering and uncertain, mixed and mingled with the slavering droolings of imbecility. He spoke a language akin to the dialects Kane had learned from friendly river folk on his wanderings, and Kane gathered that he had been bound to the stake for a long time—many moons, he whimpered in the delirium of approaching death; and all this time, inhuman, evil things had worked their monstrous will upon him. These things he mentioned by name, but Kane could make nothing of it for he used an unfamiliar term that sounded like akaana. But these things had not bound him to the stake, for the torn wretch slavered the name of Goru, who was a priest and who had drawn a cord too tight about his legs—and Kane wondered that the memory of this small pain should linger through the red mazes of agony that the dying man should whimper over it.

And to Kane's horror, the man spoke of his brother who had aided in the binding of him, and he wept with infantile sobs. Moisture formed in the empty sockets and made tears of blood. And he muttered of a spear broken long ago in some dim hunt, and while he muttered in his delirium, Kane gently cut his bonds and eased his broken body to the grass. But even at the Englishman's careful touch, the poor wretch writhed and howled like a dying dog, while blood started anew from a score of ghastly gashes, which, Kane noted, were more like the wounds made by fang and talon than by knife or spear. But at last it was done and the bloody, torn thing lay on the soft grass with Kane's old slouch hat beneath its death's-head, breathing in great, rattling gasps.

Kane poured water from his canteen between the mangled lips, and bending close, said: "Tell me more of these devils, for by the God of my people, this deed shall not go unavenged, though Satan himself bar my way."

It is doubtful if the dying man heard. But he heard something else. The macaw, with the curiosity of its breed, swept from a near-by grove and passed so close its great wings fanned Kane's hair. And at the sound of those wings, the butchered man heaved upright and screamed in a voice that haunted Kane's dreams to the day of his death: "The wings! The wings! They come again! Ahhh, mercy, the wings!"

And the blood burst in a torrent from his lips and so he died.

Kane rose and wiped the cold sweat from his forehead. The upland forest shimmered in the noonday heat. Silence lay over the land like an enchantment of dreams. Kane's brooding eyes ranged to the black, malevolent hills crouching in the distance and back to the far-away savannas. An ancient curse lay over that mysterious land and the shadow of it fell across the soul of Solomon Kane.

Tenderly he lifted the red ruin that had once pulsed with life and youth and vitality, and carried it to the edge of the glade, where arranging the cold limbs as best he might, and shuddering once again at the unnamable mutilations, he piled stones above it till even a prowling jackal would find it hard to get at the flesh below.

And he had scarcely finished when something jerked him back out of his somber broodings to a realization of his own position. A slight sound—or his own wolf-like instinct—made him whirl.

On the other side of the glade he caught a movement among the tall grasses—the glimpse of a hideous face, with an ivory ring in the flat nose, thick lips parted to reveal teeth whose filed points were apparent even at that distance, beady eyes and a low slanting forehead topped by a mop of frizzly hair. Even as the face faded from view Kane leaped back into the shelter of the ring of trees which circled the glade, and ran like a deer-hound, flitting from tree to tree and expecting at each moment to hear the exultant clamor of the warriors and to see them break cover at his back.

But soon he decided that they were content to hunt him down as certain beasts track their prey, slowly and inevitably. He hastened through the upland forest, taking advantage of every bit of cover, and he saw no more of his pursuers; yet he knew, as a hunted wolf knows, that they hovered close behind him, waiting their moment to strike him down without risk to their own hides.

Kane smiled bleakly and without mirth. If it was to be a test of endurance, he would see how savage thews compared with his own spring-steel resilience. Let night come and he might yet give them the slip. If not—Kane knew in his heart that the savage essence of his very being which chafed at his flight, would make him soon turn at bay, though his pursuers outnumbered him a hundred to one.

The sun sank westward. Kane was hungry, for he had not eaten since early morning when he wolfed down the last of his dried meat. An occasional spring had given him water, and once he thought he glimpsed the roof of a large hut far away through the trees. But he gave it a wide berth. It was hard to believe that this silent plateau was inhabited, but if it were, the natives were doubtless as ferocious as those hunting him.

Ahead of him the land grew rougher, with broken boulders and steep slopes as he neared the lower reaches of the brooding hills. And still no sight of his hunters except for faint glimpses caught by wary backward glances—a drifting shadow, the bending of the grass, the sudden straightening of a trodden twig, a rustle of leaves. Why should they be so cautious? Why did they not close in and have it over?

Night fell and Kane reached the first long slopes which led upward to the foot of the hills which now brooded black and menacing above him. They were his goal, where he hoped to shake off his persistent foes at last, yet a nameless aversion warned him away from them. They were pregnant with hidden evil, repellent as the coil of a great sleeping serpent, glimpsed in the tall grass.

Darkness fell heavily. The stars winked redly in the

thick heat of the tropic night. And Kane, halting for a moment in an unusually dense grove, beyond which the trees thinned out on the slopes, heard a stealthy movement that was not the night wind—for no breath of air stirred the heavy leaves. And even as he turned, there was a rush in the dark, under the trees.

A shadow that merged with the shadows flung itself on Kane with a bestial mouthing and a rattle of iron, and the Englishman, parrying by the gleam of the stars on the weapon, felt his assailant duck into close quarters and meet him chest to chest. Lean wiry arms locked about him, pointed teeth gnashed at him as Kane returned the fierce grapple. His tattered shirt ripped beneath a jagged edge, and by blind chance Kane found and pinioned the hand that held the iron knife, and drew his own dirk, flesh crawling in anticipation of a spear in the back.

But even as the Englishman wondered why the others did not come to their comrade's aid, he threw all of his iron muscles into the single combat. Close-clinched they swayed and writhed in the darkness, each striving to drive his blade into the other's flesh, and as the superior strength of the Puritan began to assert itself, the cannibal howled like a rabid dog, tore and bit.

A convulsive spin-wheel of effort pivoted them out into the starlit glade where Kane saw the ivory nose-ring and the pointed teeth that snapped beast-like at his throat. And simultaneously he forced back and down the hand that gripped his knife-wrist, and drove the dirk deep into the savage wrists. The warrior screamed, and the raw acrid scent of blood flooded the night air. And in that instant Kane was stunned by a sudden savage rush and beat of mighty wings that dashed him to earth, and the cannibal was torn from his grip and vanished with a scream of mortal agony. Kane leaped to his feet, shaken to his foundation. The dwindling scream of the wretched savage sounded faintly and from above him.

Straining his eyes into the skies he thought he

caught a glimpse of a shapeless and horrific Thing crossing the dim stars—in which the writhing limbs of a human mingled namelessly with great wings and a shadowy shape—but so quickly it was gone, he could not be sure.

And now he wondered if it were not all a nightmare. But groping in the grove he found the ju-ju stave with which he had parried the short stabbing spear that lay beside it. And here, if more proof was needed, was his long dirk, still stained with blood.

Wings! Wings in the night! The skeleton in the village of torn roofs—the mutilated warrior whose wounds were not made with knife or spear and who died shrieking of wings. Surely those hills were the haunt of gigantic birds who made humanity their prey. Yet if birds, why had they not wholly devoured the torn man on the stake? And Kane knew in his heart that no true bird ever cast such a shadow as he had seen flit across the stars.

He shrugged his shoulders, bewildered. The night was silent. Where were the rest of the cannibals who had followed him from their distant jungle? Had the fate of their comrade frightened them into flight? Kane looked to his pistols. Cannibals or no, he went not up into those dark hills that night.

Now he must sleep, if all the devils of the Elder World were on his track. A deep roaring to the westward warned him that beasts of prey were aroam, and he walked rapidly down the rolling slopes until he came to a dense grove some distance from that in which he had fought the cannibal. He climbed high among the great branches until he found a thick crotch that would accommodate even his tall frame. The branches above would guard him from a sudden swoop of any winged thing, and if savages were lurking near, their clamber into the tree would warn him, for he slept lightly as a cat. As for serpents and leopards, they were chances he had taken a thousand times.

Solomon Kane slept and his dreams were vague, chaotic, haunted with a suggestion of pre-human evil and which at last merged into a vision vivid as a scene in waking life. Solomon dreamed he woke with a start, drawing a pistol—for so long had his life been that of the wolf, that reaching for a weapon was his natural reaction upon waking suddenly.

His dream was that a strange, shadowy thing had perched upon a great branch close by and gazed at him with greedy, luminous yellow eyes that seared into his brain. The dream-thing was tall and lean and strangely misshapen, so blended with the shadows that it seemed a shadow itself, tangible only in the narrow yellow eyes. And Kane dreamed he waited, spellbound, while uncertainty came into those eyes and then the creature walked out on the limb as a man would walk, raised great shadowy wings, sprang into space and vanished.

Kane jerked upright, the mists of sleep fading. In the dim starlight, under the arching Gothic-like branches, the tree was empty save for himself. Then it had been a dream, after all—yet it had been so vivid, so fraught with inhuman foulness—even now a faint scent like that exuded by birds of prey seemed to linger in the air. Kane strained his ears. He heard the sighing of the night wind, the whisper of the leaves, the far-away roaring of a lion, but naught else. Again Solomon slept—while high above him a shadow wheeled against the stars, circling again and again as a vulture circles a dying wolf.

CHAPTER 2
THE BATTLE IN THE SKY

Dawn was spreading whitely over the eastern hills when Kane woke. The thought of his nightmare came to him and he wondered again at its vividness as he climbed down out of the tree. A nearby spring slaked his thirst and some fruit, rare in these highlands, eased his hunger.

Then he turned his face again to the hills. A finish fighter was Solomon Kane. Along that grim skyline dwelt some evil foe to the sons of men, and that mere fact was as much a challenge to the Puritan as had ever been a glove thrown in his face by some hot-headed gallant of Devon.

Refreshed by his night's sleep, he set out with his long easy stride, passing the grove that had witnessed the battle in the night, and coming into the region where the trees thinned at the foot of the slopes. Up these slopes he went, halting for a moment to gaze back over the way he had come. Now that he was above the plateau, he could easily make out a village in the distance—a cluster of mud-and-bamboo huts with one unusually large hut a short distance from the rest on a sort of low knoll.

And while he gazed, with a sudden rush of grisly wings the terror was upon him! Kane whirled, galvanized. All signs had pointed to the theory of a winged thing that hunted by night. He had not expected attack in broad daylight—but here a bat-like monster was swooping at him out of the very eye of the rising sun. Kane saw a spread of mighty wings, from which glared a horribly human face; then he drew and fired with unerring aim and the monster veered wildly in midair and came whirling and tumbling out of the sky to crash at his feet.

Kane leaned forward, pistol smoking in his hand, and gazed wide-eyed. Surely this thing was a demon out of the pits of hell, said the sombre mind of the Puritan; yet a leaden ball had slain it. Kane shrugged his shoulders, baffled; he had never seen aught to approach this, though all his life had fallen in strange ways.

The thing was like a man, inhumanly tall and inhumanly thin; the head was long, narrow, and hairless— the head of a predatory creature. The ears were small, close-set and queerly pointed. The eyes, set in death, were narrow, oblique and of a strange yellowish color. The nose was thin and hooked, like the beak of a bird of prey, the mouth a wide cruel gash, whose thin lips, writhed in a death snarl and flecked with foam, disclosed wolfish fangs.

The creature, which was naked and hairless, was not unlike a human being in other ways. The shoulders were broad and powerful, the neck long and lean. The arms were long and muscular, the thumb being set beside the fingers after the manner of the great apes. Fingers and thumbs were armed with heavy hooked talons. The chest was curiously misshapen, the breast-bone jutting out like the keel of a ship, the ribs curving back from it. The legs were long and wiry with huge, hand-like, prehensile feet, the great toe set opposite the rest like a man's thumb. The claws on the toes were merely long nails.

But the most curious feature of this curious creature was on its back. A pair of great wings, shaped much like the wings of a moth but with a bony frame and of leathery substance, grew from its shoulders, beginning at a point just back and above where the arms joined the shoulders, and extending half way to the narrow hips. These wings, Kane reckoned, would measure some eighteen feet from tip to tip.

He laid hold on the creature, involuntarily shuddering at the slick, hard leather-like feel of the skin, and half-lifted it. The weight was little more than half as much as it would have been in a man the same height—some six and a half feet. Evidently the bones were of a peculiar bird-like structure and the flesh consisted almost entirely of stringy muscles.

Kane stepped back, surveying the thing again. Then his dream had been no dream after all—that foul thing or another like it had in grisly reality lighted in the tree beside him—a whir of mighty wings! A sudden rush through the sky! Even as Kane whirled he realized he had committed the jungle-farer's unpardonable crime—he had allowed his astonishment and curiosity to throw him off guard. Already a winged fiend was at his throat and there was no time to draw and fire his other pistol. Kane saw, in a maze of thrashing wings, a devilish, semi-human face—he felt those wings battering at him—he felt cruel talons sink deep into his breast; then he was dragged off his feet and felt empty space beneath him.

The winged man had wrapped his limbs about the Englishman's legs, and the talons he had driven into Kane's breast muscles held like fanged vises. The wolf-like fangs drove at Kane's throat, but the Puritan gripped the bony throat and thrust back the grisly head, while with his right hand he strove to draw his dirk. The birdman was mounting slowly and a fleeting glance showed Kane that they were already high above the trees. The Englishman did not hope to survive this battle in the sky, for even if he slew his foe, he would be dashed to death in the fall. But with the innate ferocity of the fighting man he set himself grimly to take his captor with him.

Holding those keen fangs at bay, Kane managed to draw his dirk, and he plunged it deep into the body of the monster. The bat-man veered wildly and a rasping, raucous screech burst from his half-throttled throat. He floundered wildly, beating frantically with his great wings, bowing his back and twisting his head fiercely in a vain effort to free it and sink home his deadly fangs. He sank the talons of one hand agonizingly deeper and deeper into Kane's breast muscles, while with the other he tore at his foe's head and body. But the Englishman, gashed and bleeding, with the silent and tenacious savagery of a bull dog, sank his fingers deeper into the lean neck and drove his dirk home again and again, while far below awed eyes watched the fiendish battle that was raging at that dizzy height.

They had drifted out over the plateau, and the fast-weakening wings of the bat-man barely supported their weight. They were sinking earthward swiftly, but Kane, blinded with blood and battle fury, knew nothing of this. With a great piece of his scalp hanging loose, his chest and shoulders cut and ripped, the world had become a blind, red thing in which he was aware of but one sensation—the bulldog urge to kill his foe.

Now the feeble and spasmodic beating of the dying monster's wings held them hovering for an instant above a thick grove of gigantic trees, while Kane felt the grip of claws and twining limbs grow weaker and the slashing of the talons become a futile flailing.

With a last burst of power he drove the reddened dirk straight through the breastbone and felt a convulsive tremor run through the creature's frame. The great wings fell limp—and victor and vanquished dropped headlong and plummet-like earthward.

Through a red wave Kane saw the waving branches rushing up to meet him—he felt them flail his face and tear at his clothing, as still locked in that death-clinch he rushed downward through leaves which eluded his vainly grasping hand; then his head crashed against a great limb, and an endless abyss of blackness engulfed him.

CHAPTER 3
THE PEOPLE IN THE SHADOW

Through colossal, black basaltic corridors of night, Solomon Kane fled for a thousand years. Gigantic winged demons, horrific in the utter darkness, swept over him with a rush of great bat-like pinions and in the blackness he fought with them as a cornered rat fights a vampire bat, while fleshless jaws drooled fearful blasphemies and horrid secrets in his ears, and the skulls of men rolled under his groping feet.

Solomon Kane came back suddenly from the land of delirium and his first sight of sanity was that of a fat, kindly native face bending over him. Kane saw he was in a roomy, clean and well-ventilated hut, while from a cooking pot bubbling outside wafted savory scents. Kane realized he was ravenously hungry. And he was strangely weak. The hand he lifted to his bandaged head shook, and its bronze was dimmed.

The fat man and another, a tall, gaunt, grim-faced warrior, bent over him, and the fat man said: "He is awoke, Kuroba, and of sound mind." The gaunt man nodded and called something which was answered from without.

"What is this place?" asked Kane in a language he had learned that was similar to the dialect just used. "How long have I lain here?"

"This is the last village of Bogonda." The fat man pressed him back with hands as gentle as a woman's. "We found you lying beneath the trees on the slopes, badly wounded and senseless. You have raved in delirium for many days. Now eat."

A lithe young warrior entered with a wooden bowl full of steaming food and Kane ate ravenously.

"He is like a leopard, Kuroba," said the fat man admiringly. "Not one in a thousand would have lived with his wounds."

"Aye," returned the other. "And he slew the akaana that rent him, Goru."

Kane struggled to his elbows. "Goru?" he cried fiercely. "The priest who binds men to stakes for devils to eat?"

And he strove to rise so that he could strangle the fat man, but his weakness swept over him like a wave, the hut swam dizzily to his eyes and he sank back panting, where he soon fell into a sound, natural sleep.

Later he awoke and found a slim young girl, named Nayela, watching him. She fed him, and feeling much stronger, Kane asked questions which she answered shyly but intelligently.

This was Bogonda, ruled by Kuroba the chief and Goru the priest. None in Bogonda had ever seen or heard of a white man before. She counted the days

Kane had lain helpless, and he was amazed. But such a battle as he had been through was enough to kill an ordinary man. He wondered that no bones had been broken, but the girl said the branches had broken his fall and he had landed on the body of the akaana. He asked for Goru, and the fat priest came to him, bringing Kane's weapons.

"Some we found with you where you lay," said Goru, "some by the body of the akaana you slew with the weapon which speaks in fire and smoke. You must be a god—yet the gods bleed not and you have just all but died. Who are you?"

"I am no god," Kane answered, "but a man like yourself. I come from a far land amid the sea, which land, mind ye, is the fairest and noblest of all lands. My name is Solomon Kane and I am a landless wanderer. From the lips of a dying man I first heard your name. Yet your face seemeth kindly."

A shadow crossed the eyes of the shaman and he hung his head.

"Rest and grow strong, oh man, or god or whatever you be," said he, "and in time you will learn of the ancient curse that rests upon this ancient land."

And in the days that followed, while Kane recovered and grew strong with the wild beast vitality that was his, Goru and Kuroba sat and spoke to him at length, telling him many curious things.

Their tribe was not aboriginal here, but had come upon the plateau a hundred and fifty years before, giving it the name of their former home. They had once been a powerful tribe in Old Bogonda, on a great river far to the south. But tribal wars broke their power, and at last before a concerted uprising, the whole tribe gave way, and Goru repeated legends of that great flight of a thousand miles through jungle and swampland, harried at every step by cruel foes.

At last, hacking their way through a country of ferocious cannibals, they found themselves safe from man's attack—but prisoners in a trap from which neither they nor their descendants could ever escape.

They were in the horror-country of Akaana, and Goru said his ancestors came to understand the jeering laughter of the maneaters who had hounded them to the very borders of the plateau.

The Bogondi found a fertile country with good water and plenty of game. There were numbers of goats and a species of wild pig that throve here in great abundance. At first the people ate these pigs, but later they spared them for a good reason. The grasslands between plateau and jungle swarmed with antelopes, buffaloes and the like, and there were many lions. Lions also roamed the plateau, but Bogonda meant "Lionslayer" in their tongue and it was not many moons before the remnants of the great cats took to the lower levels. But it was not lions they had to fear, as Goru's ancestors soon learned.

Finding that the cannibals would not come past the savannas, they rested from their long trek and built two villages—Upper and Lower Bogonda. Kane was in Upper Bogonda; he had seen the ruins of the lower village. But soon they found that they had strayed into a country of nightmares with dripping fangs and talons. They heard the beat of mighty wings at night, and saw horrific shadows cross the stars and loom against the moon. Children began to disappear and at last a young hunter strayed off into the hills, where night overtook him. And in the gray light of dawn a mangled, half-devoured corpse fell from the skies into the village street and a whisper of ogreish laughter from high above froze the horrified on-lookers. Then a little later the full horror of their position burst upon the Bogondi.

At first the winged men were afraid of the newcomers. They hid themselves and ventured from their caverns only at night. Then they grew bolder. In the full daylight, a warrior shot one with an arrow, but the fiends had learned they could slay a human, and its death scream brought a score of the devils dropping from the skies, who tore the slayer to pieces in full sight of the tribe.

The Bogondi then prepared to leave that devil's country and a hundred warriors went up into the hills to find a pass. They found steep walls, up which a man must climb laboriously, and they found the cliffs honeycombed with caves where the winged men dwelt.

Then was fought the first pitched battle between men and bat-men, and it resulted in a crushing victory for the monsters. The bows and spears of the natives proved futile before the swoops of the taloned fiends, and of all that hundred that went up into the hills, not one survived; for the akaanas hunted down those that fled and dragged down the last one within bowshot of the upper village.

Then it was that the Bogondi, seeing they could not hope to win through the hills, sought to fight their way out again the way they had come. But a great horde of cannibals met them in the grasslands, and in a great battle that lasted nearly all day, hurled them back, broken and defeated. And Goru said while the battle raged, the skies were thronged with hideous shapes, circling above and laughing their fearful mirth to see men die wholesale.

So the survivors of those two battles, licking their wounds, bowed to the inevitable with the fatalistic philosophy of the savage. Some fifteen hundred men, women and children remained, and they built their huts, tilled the soil and lived stolidly in the shadow of the nightmare.

In those days there were many of the bird-people, and they might have wiped out the Bogondi utterly, had they wished. No one warrior could cope with an akaana, for he was stronger than a human, he struck as a hawk strikes, and if he missed, his wings carried him out of reach of a counterblow.

Here Kane interrupted to ask why the Bogondi did not make war on the demons with arrows. But Goru answered that it took a quick and accurate archer to strike an akaana in midair at all, and so tough were their hides that unless the arrow struck squarely it would not penetrate. Kane knew that the natives were very indifferent bowmen and that they pointed their shafts with chipped stone, bone, or hammered iron almost as soft as copper; he thought of Poitiers and Agincourt and wished grimly for a file of stout English archers—or a rank of musketeers.

But Goru said the akaanas did not seem to wish to destroy the Bogondi utterly. Their chief food consisted of the little pigs which then swarmed the plateau, and young goats. Sometimes they went out on the savannas for antelope, but they distrusted the open country and feared the lions. Nor did they haunt the jungles beyond, for the trees grew too close for the spread of their wings. They kept to the hills and the plateau—and what lay beyond those hills none in Bogonda knew.

The akaanas allowed the Bogondi to inhabit the plateau much as men allow wild animals to thrive, or stock lakes with fish—for their own pleasure. The bat-people, said Goru, had a strange and grisly sense of humor which was tickled by the sufferings of a howling human. Those grim hills had echoed to cries that turned men's hearts to ice.

But for many years, Goru said, once the Bogondi learned not to resist their masters, the akaanas were content to snatch up a baby from time to time, or devour a young girl strayed from the village or a youth whom night caught outside the walls. The bat-folk distrusted the village; they circled high above it but did not venture within. There the Bogondi were safe until late years.

Goru said that the akaanas were fast dying out; once there had been hope that the remnants of his race would outlast them—in which event, he said fatalistically, the cannibals would undoubtedly come up from the jungle and put the survivors in their cooking pots. Now he doubted if there were more than a hundred and fifty akaanas altogether. Kane asked him why did not the warriors then sally forth on a great hunt and destroy the devils utterly, and

Goru smiled a bitter smile and repeated his remarks about the prowess of the bat-people in battle. Moreover, said he, the whole tribe of Bogonda numbered only about four hundred souls now, and the bat-people were their only protection against the cannibals to the west.

Goru said the tribe had thinned more in the past thirty years than in all the years previous. As the numbers of the akaanas dwindled, their hellish savagery increased. They seized more and more of the Bogondi to torture and devour in their grim black caves high up in the hills, and Goru spoke of sudden raids on hunting parties and toilers in the plantain fields, and of the nights made ghastly by horrible screams and gibberings from the dark hills, and blood-freezing laughter that was half-human; of dismembered limbs and gory grinning heads flung from the skies to fall in the shuddering village, and of grisly feasts among the stars.

Then came drouth, Goru said, and a great famine. Many of the springs dried up and the crops of rice and yams and plantains failed. The gnus, deer, and buffaloes which had formed the main part of Bogonda's meat diet withdrew to the jungle in quest of water, and the lions, their hunger overcoming their fear of man, ranged into the uplands. Many of the tribe died, and the rest were driven by hunger to eat the pigs which were the natural prey of the bat-people. This angered the akaanas and thinned the pigs. Famine, Bogondi, and the lions destroyed all the goats and half the pigs.

At last the famine was past, but the damage was done. Of all the great droves which once swarmed the plateau, only a remnant was left, and these were hard to catch. The Bogondi had eaten the pigs, so the akaanas ate the Bogondi. Life became a hell for the humans, and the lower village, numbering now only some hundred and fifty souls, rose in revolt. Driven to frenzy by repeated outrages, they turned on their masters. An akaana lighting in the very streets to steal a child was set on and shot to death with arrows. And the people of Lower Bogonda drew into their huts and waited for their doom.

And in the night, said Goru, it came. The akaanas had overcome their distrust of the huts. The full flock of them swarmed down from the hills, and Upper Bogonda awoke to hear the fearful cataclysm of screams and blasphemies that marked the end of the other village. All night Goru's people had lain sweating in terror, not daring to move, harkening to the howling and gibbering that rent the night. At last these sounds ceased, Goru said, wiping the cold sweat from his brow, but sounds of grisly and obscene feasting still haunted the night with demon's mockery.

In the early dawn Goru's people saw the hell-flock winging back to their hills, like demons flying back to hell through the dawn. They flew slowly and heavily, like gorged vultures. Later the people dared to steal down to the accursed village, and what they found there sent them shrieking away. And to that day, Goru said, no man passed within three bow shots of that silent horror. And Kane nodded in understanding, his cold eyes more sombre than ever.

For many days after that, Goru said the people waited in quaking fear. Finally in desperation of fear, which breeds unspeakable cruelty, the tribe cast lots and the loser was bound to a stake between the two villages, in hopes that the akaanas would recognize this as a token of submission so that the people of Bogonda might escape the fate of their kinsmen. The custom, said Goru, had been borrowed from the cannibals who in old times worshipped the akaanas and offered a human sacrifice at each moon. But chance had shown them that the akaanas could be killed, so they ceased to worship them—at least that was Goru's deduction, and he explained at much length that no mortal thing is worthy of real adoration, however evil or powerful it may be.

His own ancestors had made occasional sacrifices

to placate the winged devils, but until lately it had not been a regular custom. Now it was necessary; the akaanas expected it, and each moon they chose from their waning numbers a strong young man or a girl whom they bound to the stake.

Kane watched Goru's face closely as he spoke of his sorrow for this unspeakable necessity, and the Englishman realized that the priest was sincere. Kane shuddered at the thought of a tribe of human beings thus passing slowly but surely into the maws of a race of monsters.

Kane spoke of the wretch he had seen, and Goru nodded, pain in his soft eyes. For a day and a night he had been hanging there, while the akaanas glutted their vile torture-lust on his quivering, agonized flesh. Thus far the sacrifices had kept doom from the village. The remaining pigs furnished sustenance for the dwindling akaanas, together with an occasional baby snatched up, and they were content to have their nameless sport with the single victim each moon.

A thought came to Kane.

"The cannibals never came up into the plateau?"

Goru shook his head; safe in their jungle, they never raided past the savannas.

"But they hunted me to the very foot of the hills."

Again Goru shook his head. There was only one cannibal; they had found his footprints. Evidently a single warrior, bolder than the rest, had allowed his passion for the chase to overcome his fear of the grisly plateau and had paid the penalty. Kane's teeth came together with a vicious snap which ordinarily took the place of profanity with him. He was stung by the thought of fleeing so long from a single enemy. No wonder that enemy had followed so cautiously, waiting until dark to attack. But, asked Kane, why had the akaana seized the cannibal instead of himself—and why had he not been attacked by the bat-man who alighted in his tree that night?

The cannibal was bleeding, Goru answered. The scent called the bat-fiend to attack, for they scented raw blood as far as vultures. And they were very wary. They had never seen a man like Kane, who showed no fear. Surely they had decided to spy on him, take him off guard before they struck.

Who were these creatures? Kane asked. Goru shrugged his shoulders. They were there when his ancestors came, who had never heard of them before they saw them. There was no intercourse with the cannibals, so they could learn nothing from them. The akaanas lived in caves, naked like beasts; they knew nothing of fire and ate only fresh, raw meat. But they had a language of a sort and acknowledged a king among them. Many died in the great famine when the stronger ate the weaker. They were vanishing swiftly; of late years no females or young had been observed among them. When these males died at last, there would be no more akaanas; but Bogonda, observed Goru, was doomed already, unless—he looked strangely and wistfully at Kane. But the Puritan was deep in thought.

Among the swarm of native legends he had heard on his wanderings, one now stood out. Long, long ago, an old, old ju-ju man had told him, winged devils came flying out of the north and passed over his country, vanishing in the maze of the jungle-haunted south. And the ju-ju man related an old, old legend concerning these creatures—that once they had abode in myriad numbers far on a great lake of bitter water many moons to the north, and ages and ages ago a chieftain and his warriors fought them with bows and arrows and slew many, driving the rest into the south. The name of the chief was N'Yasunna and he owned a great war canoe with many oars driving it swiftly through the bitter water.

And now a cold wind blew suddenly on Solomon Kane, as if from a Door opened suddenly on Outer gulfs of Time and Space. For now he realized the truth of that garbled myth, and the truth of an older, grimmer legend. For what was the great bitter lake but the Mediterranean Ocean and who was the chief

N'Yasunna but the hero Jason, who conquered the harpies and drove them—not alone into the Strophades Isles but into Africa as well? The old pagan tale was true then, Kane thought dizzily, shrinking aghast from the strange realm of grisly possibilities this opened up. For if this myth of the harpies were a reality, what of the other legends—the Hydra, the centaurs, the chimera, Medusa, Pan, and the satyrs?

All those myths of antiquity—behind them did there lie and lurk nightmare realities with slavering fangs and talons steeped in shuddersome evil? Africa, the Dark Continent, land of shadows and horror, of bewitchment and sorcery, into which all evil things had been banished before the growing light of the western world!

Kane came out of his reveries with a start. Goru was tugging gently and timidly at his sleeve.

"Save us from the akaanas!" said Goru. "If you be not a god, there is the power of a god in you! You bear in your hand the mighty ju-ju stave which has in times gone by been the scepter of fallen empires and the staff of mighty priests. And you have weapons which speak death in fire and smoke—for our young men watched and saw you slay two akaanas. We will make you king—god—what you will! More than a moon has passed since you came into Bogonda and the time for the sacrifice is gone by, but the bloody stake stands bare. The akaanas shun the village where you lie; they steal no more babes from us. We have thrown off their yoke because our trust is in you!"

Kane clasped his temples with his hands. "You know not what you ask!" he cried. "God knoweth it is in my deepest heart to rid the land of this evil, but I am no god. With my pistols I can slay a few of the fiends, but I have but a little powder left. Had I great store of powder and ball, and the musket I shattered in the vampire-haunted Hills of the Dead, then indeed would there be a rare hunting. But even if I slew all those fiends, what of the cannibals?"

"They too will fear you!" cried old Kuroba, while

the girl Nayela and the lad, Loga, who was to have been the next sacrifice, gazed at him with their souls in their eyes. Kane dropped his chin on his fist and sighed.

"Yet will I stay here in Bogonda all the rest of my life if ye think I be protection to the people."

So Solomon Kane stayed at the village of Bogonda of the Shadow. The people were a kindly folk, whose natural sprightliness and fun-loving spirits were subdued and saddened by long dwelling in the Shadow. But now they had taken new heart by the Englishman's coming, and it wrenched Kane's heart to note the pathetic trust they placed in him. Now they sang in the plantain fields and danced about the fire, and gazed at him with adoring faith in their eyes. But Kane, cursing his own helplessness, knew how futile would be his fancied protection if the winged fiends swept suddenly out of the skies.

But he stayed in Bogonda. In his dreams the gulls wheeled above the cliffs of old Devon carved in the clean, blue, wind-whipped skies, and in the day the call of the unknown lands beyond Bogonda clawed at his heart with fierce yearning. But he abode in Bogonda and racked his brains for a plan. He sat and gazed for hours at the ju-ju stave, hoping in desperation that black magic would aid him, where his mind failed. But N'Longa's ancient gift gave him no aid. Once he had summoned the Slave Coast shaman to him across leagues of intervening space—but it was only when confronted with supernatural manifestations that N'Longa could come to him, and these harpies were not supernatural.

The germ of an idea began to grow at the back of Kane's mind, but he discarded it. It had to do with a great trap—and how could the akaanas be trapped? The roaring of lions played a grim accompaniment to his brooding meditations. As man dwindled on the plateau, the hunting beasts who feared only the spears of the hunters were beginning to gather. Kane laughed bitterly. It was not lions, that might be hunted down and slain singly, that he had to deal with.

At some little distance from the village stood the great hut of Goru, once a council hall. This hut was full of many strange fetishes which, Goru said with a helpless wave of his fat hands, were strong magic against evil spirits but scant protection against winged hellions of gristle and bone and flesh.

CHAPTER 4
THE MADNESS OF SOLOMON

Kane woke suddenly from a dreamless sleep. A hideous medley of screams burst horrific in his ears. Outside his hut, people were dying in the night, horribly, as cattle die in the shambles. He had slept, as always, with his weapons buckled on him. Now he bounded to the door, and something fell mouthing and slavering at his feet to grasp his knees in a convulsive grin and gibber incoherent pleas.

In the faint light of a smoldering fire near by, Kane in horror recognized the face of the youth Loga, now frightfully torn and drenched in blood, already freezing into a death mask. The night was full of fearful sounds, inhuman howlings mingled with the whisper of mighty wings, the tearing of thatch and a ghastly demon-laughter. Kane freed himself from the locked dead arms and sprang to the dying fire. He could make out only a confused and vague maze of fleeing forms and darting shapes, the shift and blur of dark wings against the stars.

He snatched up a brand and thrust it against the thatch of his hut—and as the flame leaped up and showed him the scene he stood frozen and aghast. Red, howling doom had fallen on Bogonda. Winged monsters raced screaming through her streets, wheeled above the heads of the fleeing people, or tore apart the hut thatches to get at the gibbering victims within.

With a choked cry the Englishman woke from his trance of horror, drew and fired at a darting flame-eyed shadow which fell at his feet with a shattered skull. And Kane gave tongue to one deep, fierce roar and bounded into the melee, all the berserk fury of his heathen Saxon ancestors bursting into terrible being.

Dazed and bewildered by the sudden attack, cowed by long years of submission, the Bogondi were incapable of combined resistance and for the most part died like sheep. Some maddened by desperation, fought back, but their arrows went wild or glanced from the tough wings while the devilish agility of the creatures made spear thrust and ax stroke uncertain. Leaping from the ground they avoided the blows of their victims and, sweeping down upon their shoulders, dashed them to earth where fang and talon did their crimson work.

Kane saw old Kuroba, gaunt and bloodstained, at bay against a hut wall with his foot on the neck of a monster who had not been quick enough. The grim-faced old chief wielded a two-handed ax in great sweeping blows that for the moment held back the screeching onset of half a dozen of the devils. Kane was leaping to his aid when a low, pitiful whimper checked him. The girl Nayela writhed weakly, prone in the bloody dust, while on her back a vulture-like thing crouched and tore. Her dulling eyes sought the face of the Englishman in anguished appeal.

Kane ripped out a bitter oath and fired point blank. The winged devil pitched backward with an abhorrent screeching and a wild flutter of dying wings, and Kane bent to the dying girl. She whimpered and kissed his hands with uncertain lips as he cradled her head in his arms. Her eyes set.

Kane laid the body gently down, looking for Kuroba. He saw only a huddled cluster of grisly shapes that sucked and tore at something between them. And Kane went mad. With a scream that cut through the inferno he bounded up, slaying even as he rose. Even in the act of lunging up from bent knee he drew and thrust, transfixing a vulture-like throat. Then whipping out his rapier as the thing floundered and twitched in its death struggle, the raging Puritan charged forward seeking new victims.

On all sides of him the people of Bogonda were dying hideously. They fought futilely or they fled and the demons coursed them down as a hawk courses a hare. They ran into the huts and the fiends rent the thatch or burst the door, and what took place in those huts was mercifully hidden from Kane's eyes.

And to the frantic Puritan's horror-distorted brain it seemed that he alone was responsible. The Bogondi had trusted him to save them. They had withheld the sacrifice and defied their grim masters. Now they were paying the horrible penalty and he was unable to save them. In the agony-dimmed eyes turned toward him, Kane quaffed the black dregs of the bitter cup. It was not anger or the vindictiveness of fear. It was hurt and a stunned reproach. He was their god and he had failed them.

Now he ravened through the massacre and the fiends avoided him, turning to the easy victims. But Kane was not to be denied. In a red haze that was not of the burning hut, he saw a culminating horror; a harpy gripped a writhing naked thing that had been a woman, and the wolfish fangs gorged deep. As Kane sprang, thrusting, the bat-man dropped his yammering, mowing prey and soared aloft. But Kane dropped his rapier and with the bound of a blood-mad panther caught the demon's throat and locked his iron legs about its lower body.

Once again he found himself battling in midair, but this time close above the hut roofs. Terror had entered the cold brain of the harpy. He did not fight to hold and slay; he wished only to be rid of this silent, clinging thing that stabbed so savagely for his life. He floundered wildly, screaming abhorrently and thrashing with his wings, then as Kane's dirk bit deeper, dipped suddenly sidewise and fell headlong.

The thatch of a hut broke their fall, and Kane and the dying harpy crashed through to land on a writhing mass on the hut floor. In the lurid flickering of the burning hut outside that vaguely lighted the hut into which he had fallen, Kane saw a deed of brain-shaking horror being enacted—red-dripping fangs in a yawning gash of a mouth, and a crimson travesty of a human form that still writhed with agonized life. Then, in the maze of madness that held him, his steel fingers closed on the fiend's throat in a grip that no tearing of talons or hammering of wings could loosen, until he felt the horrid life flow out from under his fingers and the bony neck hung broken.

Outside, the red madness of slaughter continued. Kane bounded up, his hand closing blindly on the haft of some weapon, and as he leaped from the hut a harpy soared from under his very feet. It was an ax that Kane had snatched up, and he dealt a stroke that spattered the demon's brains like water. He sprang forward, stumbling over bodies and parts of bodies, blood streaming from a dozen wounds, and then halted, baffled and screaming with rage.

The bat-people were taking to the air. No longer would they face this strange madman who in his insanity was more terrible than they. But they went not alone into the upper regions. In their lustful talons they bore writhing, screaming forms, and Kane, raging to and fro with his dripping ax, found himself alone in a corpse-choked village.

He threw back his head to shriek his hate at the fiends above him and he felt warm, thick drops fall into his face, while the shadowy skies were filled with screams of agony and the laughter of monsters.

As the sounds of that ghastly feast in the skies filled the night and the blood that rained from the stars fell into his face, Kane's last vestige of reason snapped. He gibbered to and fro, screaming chaotic blasphemies.

And was he not a symbol of Man, staggering among the tooth-marked bones and severed grinning heads of humans, brandishing a futile ax, and screaming incoherent hate at the grisly, winged shapes of Night that make him their prey, chuckling in demoniac triumph above him and dripping into his mad eyes the pitiful blood of their human victims?

CHAPTER 5
THE CONQUEROR

A shuddering, white-faced dawn crept over the black hills to shiver above the red shambles that had been the village of Bogonda. The huts stood intact, except for the one which had sunk to smoldering coals, but the thatches of many were torn. Dismembered bones, half or wholly stripped of flesh, lay in the streets, and some were splintered as though they had been dropped from a great height.

It was a realm of the dead where was but one sign of life. Solomon Kane leaned on his blood-clotted ax and gazed upon the scene with dull, mad eyes. He was grimed and clotted with half-dried blood from long gashes on chest, face, and shoulders, but he paid no heed to his hurts.

The people of Bogonda had not died alone. Seventeen harpies lay among the bones. Six of these Kane had slain. The rest had fallen before the frantic dying desperation of the Bogondi. But it was poor toll to take in return. Of the four hundred-odd people of Upper Bogonda, not one had lived to see the dawn. And the harpies were gone—back to their caves in the black hills, gorged to repletion.

With slow, mechanical steps Kane went about gathering up his weapons. He found his sword, dirk, pistols, and the ju-ju stave. He left the main village and went up the slope to the great hut of Goru. And there he halted, stung by a new horror. The ghastly humor of the harpies had prompted a delicious jest. Above the hut door stared the severed head of Goru. The fat cheeks were shrunken, the lips lolled in an aspect of horrified idiocy, and the eyes stared like a hurt child. And in those dead eyes Kane saw wonder and reproach.

Kane looked at the shambles that had been Bogonda, and he looked at the death mask of Goru. And he lifted his clenched fists above his head, and with glaring eyes raised and writhing lips flecked with froth, he cursed the sky and the earth and the spheres above and below. He cursed the cold stars, the blazing sun, the mocking moon, and the whisper of the wind. He cursed all fates and destinies, all that he had loved or hated, the silent cities beneath the seas, the past ages and the future eons. In one soul-shaking burst of blasphemy he cursed the gods and devils who make mankind their sport, and he cursed Man who lives blindly on and blindly offers his back to the iron-hoofed feet of his gods.

Then as breath failed he halted, panting. From the lower reaches sounded the deep roaring of a lion and into the eyes of Solomon Kane came a crafty gleam. He stood long, as one frozen, and out of his madness grew a desperate plan. And he silently recanted his blasphemy, for if the brazen-hoofed gods made Man for their sport and play-thing, they also gave him a brain that holds craft and cruelty greater than any other living thing.

"There you shall bide," said Solomon Kane to the head of Goru. "The sun will wither you and the cold dews of night will shrivel you. But I will keep the kites from you and your eyes shall see the fall of your slayers. Aye, I could not save the people of Bogonda, but by the God of my race, I can avenge them. Man is the sport and sustenance of titanic beings of Night and Horror whose giant wings hover ever above him. But even evil things may come to an end—and watch ye, Goru."

In the days that followed Kane labored mightily,

beginning with the first gray light of dawn and toiling on past sunset, into the white moonlight till he fell and slept the sleep of utter exhaustion. He snatched food as he worked and he gave his wounds absolutely no heed, scarcely being aware that they healed of themselves. He went down into the lower levels and cut bamboo, great stacks of long, tough stalks. He cut thick branches of trees, and tough vines to serve as ropes.

With this material he reinforced the walls and roof of Goru's hut. He set the bamboos deep in the earth, hard against the wall, and interwove and twined them, binding them fast with the vines that were pliant and tough as cords. The long branches he made fast along the thatch, binding them close together. When he had finished, an elephant could scarcely have burst through the walls.

The lions had come into the plateau in great numbers and the herds of little pigs dwindled fast. Those the lions spared, Kane slew, and tossed to the jackals. This racked Kane's heart, for he was a kindly man and this wholesale slaughter, even of pigs who would fall prey to hunting beasts anyhow, grieved him. But it was part of his plan of vengeance, and he steeled his heart.

The days stretched into weeks. Kane toiled by day and night, and between his stints he talked to the shriveled, mummied head of Goru, whose eyes, strangely enough, did not change in the blaze of the sun or the haunt of the moon, but retained their lifelike expression. When the memory of those lunacy-haunted days had become only a vague nightmare, Kane wondered if, as it had seemed to him, Goru's dried lips had moved in answer, speaking strange and mysterious things.

Kane saw the akaanas wheeling against the sky at a distance, but they did not come near, even when he slept in the great hut, pistols at hand. They feared his power to deal death with smoke and thunder.

At first he noted that they flew sluggishly, gorged

with the flesh they had eaten on that red night, and the bodies they had borne to their caves. But as the weeks passed they appeared leaner and leaner and ranged far afield in search of food. And Kane laughed, deeply and madly.

This plan of his would never have worked before, but now there were no humans to fill the bellies of the harpy-folk. And there were no more pigs. In all the plateau there were no creatures for the bat-people to eat. Why they did not range east of the hills, Kane thought he knew. That must be a region of thick jungle like the country to the west. He saw them fly into the grassland for antelopes and he saw the lions take toll of them. After all, the akaanas were weak beings among the hunters, strong enough only to slay pigs and deer—and humans.

At last they began to soar close to him at night, and he saw their greedy eyes glaring at him through the gloom. He judged the time was ripe. Huge buffaloes, too big and ferocious for the bat-people to slay, had strayed up into the plateau to ravage the deserted fields of the dead Bogondi. Kane cut one of these out of the herd and drove him, with shouts and volleys of stones, to the hut of Goru. It was a tedious, dangerous task, and time and again Kane barely escaped the surly bull's sudden charges, but persevered and at last shot the beast before the hut.

A strong west wind was blowing and Kane flung handfuls of blood into the air for the scent to waft to the harpies in the hills. He cut the bull to pieces and carried its quarters into the hut, then managed to drag the huge trunk itself inside. Then he retired into the thick trees nearby and waited.

He had not long to wait. The morning air filled suddenly with the beat of many wings, and a hideous flock alighted before the hut of Goru. All of the beasts—or men—seemed to be there, and Kane gazed in wonder at the tall, strange creatures, so like to humanity and yet so unlike—the veritable demons of priestly legend. They folded their wings like cloaks about them as they walked upright, and they talked to one another in a strident, crackling voice that had nothing of the human in it.

No, Kane decided, these things were not men. They were the materialization of some ghastly jest of Nature—some travesty of the world's infancy when Creation was an experiment. Perhaps they were the offspring of a forbidden and obscene mating of man and beast; more likely they were a freakish offshoot on the branch of evolution—for Kane had long ago dimly sensed a truth in the heretical theories of the ancient philosophers, that Man is but a higher beast. And if Nature made many strange beasts in the past ages, why should she not have experimented with monstrous forms of mankind? Surely Man as Kane knew him was not the first of his breed to walk the earth, nor yet to be the last.

Now the harpies hesitated, with their natural distrust for a building, and some soared to the roof and tore at the thatch. But Kane had built well. They returned to earth and at last, driven beyond endurance by the smell of raw blood and the sight of the flesh within, one of them ventured inside. In an instant all were crowded into the great hut, tearing ravenously at the meat, and when the last one was within, Kane reached out a hand and jerked a long vine which tripped the catch that held the door he had built. It fell with a crash, and the bar he had fashioned dropped into place. That door would hold against the charge of a wild bull.

Kane came from his cover and scanned the sky. Some hundred and forty harpies had entered the hut. He saw no more winging through the skies and believed it safe to suppose he had the whole flock trapped. Then with a cruel, brooding smile, Kane struck flint and steel to a pile of dead leaves next the wall. Within sounded an uneasy mumbling as the creatures realized that they were prisoners. A thin wisp of smoke curled upward and a flicker of red followed it; the whole heap burst into flame and the dry bamboo caught.

A few moments later the whole side of the wall was ablaze. The fiends inside scented the smoke and grew restless. Kane heard them cackling wildly and clawing at the walls. He grinned savagely, bleakly and without mirth. Now a veer of the wind drove the flames around the wall and up over the thatch—with a roar the whole hut caught and leaped into flame.

From within sounded a fearful pandemonium. Kane heard bodies crash against the walls, which shook to the impact but held. The horrid screams were music to his soul, and brandishing his arms, he answered them with screams of fearful, soul-shaking laughter. The cataclysm of horror rose unbearably, paling the tumult of the flames. Then it dwindled to a medley of strangled gibbering and gasps as the flames ate in and the smoke thickened. An intolerable scent of burning flesh pervaded the atmosphere, and had there been room in Kane's brain for aught else than insane triumph, he would have shuddered to realize that the scent was of that nauseating and indescribable odor that only human flesh emits when burning.

From the thick cloud of smoke, Kane saw a mowing, gibbering thing emerge through the shredding roof and flap slowly and agonizingly upward on fearfully burned wings. Calmly he aimed and fired, and the scorched and blinded thing tumbled back into the flaming mass just as the walls crashed in. To Kane it seemed that Goru's crumbling face, vanishing in the smoke, split suddenly in a wide grin and a sudden shout of exultant human laughter mingled eerily in the roar of the flames. But the smoke and insane brain play queer tricks.

Kane stood with the ju-ju stave in one hand the smoking pistol in the other, above the smoldering ruins that hid forever from the sight of man the last of those terrible, semi-human monsters whom another hero had banished from Europe in an unknown age. Kane stood, an unconscious statue of triumph—cold-eyed, dominant, the supreme fighting man.

Smoke curled upward into the morning sky, and the roaring of foraging lions shook the plateau. Slowly, like light breaking through mists, sanity returned to him.

"The light of God's morning enters even into dark and lonesome lands," said Solomon Kane sombrely. "Evil rules in the waste lands of the earth, but even evil may come to an end. Dawn follows midnight and even in this lost land the shadows shrink. Strange are Thy'ways, oh God of my people, and who am I to question Thy wisdom? My feet have fallen in evil ways but Thou hast brought me forth scatheless and hast made me a scourge for the Powers of Evil. Over the souls of men spread the condor wings of colossal monsters and all manner of evil things prey upon the heart and soul and body of Man. Yet it may be in some far day the shadows shall fade and the Prince of Darkness be chained forever in his hell. And till then mankind can but stand up stoutly to the monsters in his own heart and without, and with the aid of God he may yet triumph."

And Solomon Kane looked up into the silent hills and felt the silent call of the hills and the unguessed distances beyond; and Solomon Kane shifted his belt, took his staff firmly in his hand and turned his face eastward.

THE FOOTFALLS WITHIN

Solomon Kane gazed sombrely at the native woman who lay dead at his feet. Little more than a girl she was, but her wasted limbs and staring eyes showed that she had suffered much before death brought her merciful relief. Kane noted the chain galls on her limbs, the deep crisscrossed sears on her back, the mark of the yoke on her neck. His cold eyes deepened strangely, showing chill glints and lights like clouds passing across depths of ice.

"Even into this lonesome land they come," he muttered. "I had not thought—"

He raised his head and gazed eastward. Black dots against the blue wheeled and circled.

"The kites mark their trail," muttered the tall Englishman. "Destruction goeth before them and death followeth after. Wo unto ye, sons of iniquity, for the wrath of God is upon ye. The cords be loosed on the iron necks of the hounds of hate and the bow of vengeance is strung. Ye are proud-stomached and strong, and the people cry out beneath your feet, but retribution cometh in the blackness of midnight and the redness of dawn."

He shifted the belt that held his heavy pistols and the keen dirk, instinctively touched the long rapier at his hip, and went stealthily but swiftly eastward. A cruel anger burned in his deep eyes like blue volcanic fires burning beneath leagues of ice, and the hand that gripped his long, cat-headed stave hardened into iron.

After some hours of steady striding, he came within

hearing of the slave train that wound its laborious way through the jungle. The piteous cries of the slaves, the shouts and curses of the drivers, and the cracking of the whips came plainly to his ears. Another hour brought him even with them, and gliding along through the jungle parallel to the trail taken by the slavers, he spied upon them safely. Kane had fought Indians in Darien and had learned much of their woodcraft.

More than a hundred natives, young men and women, staggered along the trail, stark naked and made fast together by cruel yoke-like affairs of wood. These yokes, rough and heavy, fitted over their necks and linked them together, two by two. The yokes were in turn fettered together, making one long chain. Of the drivers there were fifteen Arabs and some seventy negro warriors, whose weapons and fantastic apparel showed them to be of some eastern tribe—one of those tribes subjugated and made Moslems and allies by the conquering Arabs.

Five Arabs walked ahead of the train with some thirty of their warriors, and five brought up the rear with the rest of the negro warriors. The rest marched beside the staggering slaves, urging them along with shouts and curses and with long, cruel whips which brought spurts of blood at almost every blow. These slavers were fools as well as rogues, reflected Kane—not more than half of them would survive the hardships of the trek to the coast.

He wondered at the presence of these raiders, for this country lay far to the south of the districts which they usually frequented. But avarice can drive men far, as the Englishman knew. He had dealt with these gentry of old. Even as he watched, old scars burned in his back—scars made by Moslem whips in a Turkish galley. And deeper still burned Kane's unquenchable hate.

The Puritan followed, shadowing his foes like a ghost, and as he stole through the jungle, he racked his brain for a plan. How might he prevail against that horde? All of the Arabs and many of their allies were armed with guns—long, clumsy firelock affairs, it is true, but guns just the same, enough to awe any tribe of natives who might oppose them. Some carried in their wide girdles long, silver-chased pistols of more effective pattern—flintlocks of Moorish and Turkish make.

Kane followed like a brooding ghost and his rage and hatred ate into his soul like a canker. Each crack of the whips was like a blow on his own shoulders. The heat and cruelty of the tropics play queer tricks. Ordinary passions become monstrous things; irritation runs to a berserker rage; anger flames into unexpected madness and men kill in a red mist of passion, and wonder, aghast, afterward.

The fury Solomon Kane felt would have been enough at any time and in any place to shake a man to his foundation. Now it assumed monstrous proportions, so that Kane shivered as if with a chill; iron claws scratched at his brain and he saw the slaves and the slavers through a crimson mist. Yet he might not have put his hate-born insanity into action had it not been for a mishap.

One of the slaves, a slim young girl, suddenly faltered and slipped to he earth, dragging her yoke-mate with her. A tall, hook-nosed Arab yelled savagely and lashed her viciously. Her yoke-mate staggered partly up, but the girl remained prone, writhing weakly beneath the lash, but evidently unable to rise. She whimpered pitifully between her parched lips, and other slavers came about her, their whips descending on her quivering flesh in slashes of red agony.

A half hour of rest and a little water would have revived her, but the Arabs had no time to spare. Solomon, biting his arm until his teeth met in the flesh as he fought for control, thanked God that the lashing had ceased and steeled himself for the swift flash of the dagger that would put the child beyond torment. But the Arabs were in a mood for sport. Since the girl would fetch them no profit on the market block, they would utilize her for their pleasure—and their humor was such as to turn men's blood to icy water.

A shout from the first whipper brought the rest crowding around, their bearded faces split in grins of delighted anticipation, while their savage allies edged nearer, their eyes gleaming. The wretched slaves realized their masters' intentions and a chorus of pitiful cries rose from them.

Kane, sick with horror, realized, too, that the girl's was to be no easy death. He knew what the tall Moslem intended to do, as he stooped over her with a keen dagger such as the Arabs used for skinning game. Madness overcame the Englishman. He valued his own life little; he had risked it without thought for the sake of a pagan child or a small animal. Yet he would not have premeditatedly thrown away his one hope of succoring the wretches in the train. But he acted without conscious thought. A pistol was smoking in his hand and the tall butcher was down in the dust of the trail with his brains oozing out, before Kane realized what he had done.

He was almost as astonished as the Arabs, who stood frozen for a moment and then burst into a medley of yells. Several threw up their clumsy firelocks and sent their heavy balls crashing through the trees, and the rest, thinking no doubt that they were ambushed, led a reckless charge into the jungle. The bold suddenness of that move was Kane's undoing. Had they hesitated a moment longer he might have faded away unobserved, but as it was he saw no choice but to meet them openly and sell his life as highly as he could.

And indeed it was with a certain ferocious fascination that he faced his howling attackers. They halted in sudden amazement as the tall, grim Englishman stepped from behind his tree, and in that instant one of them died with a bullet from Kane's remaining pistol in his heart. Then with yells of savage rage they flung themselves on their lone defier.

Solomon Kane placed his back against a huge tree

and his long rapier played a shining wheel about him.
An Arab and three of his equally fierce allies were
hacking at him with their heavy curved blades while
the rest milled about, snarling like wolves, as they
sought to drive in blade or ball without maiming one
of their own number.

The flickering rapier parried the whistling simitars
and the Arab died on its point, which seemed to hesitate in his heart only an instant before it pierced the
brain of a sword-wielding warrior. Another attacker
dropped his sword and leaped in to grapple at close
quarters. He was disembowled by the dirk in Kane's
left hand, and the others gave back in sudden fear. A
heavy ball smashed against the tree close to Kane's
head and he tensed himself to spring and die in the
thick of them. Then their sheikh lashed them on with
his long whip, and Kane heard him shouting fiercely
for his warriors to take the infidel alive. Kane answered the command with a sudden cast of his dirk,
which hummed so close to the sheikh's head that it slit
his turban and sank deep in the shoulder of one behind
him.

The sheikh drew his silver-chased pistols, threatening his own men with death if they did not take this
fierce opponent, and they charged in again desperately. One of the warriors ran full upon Kane's sword
and an Arab behind the fellow, with ruthless craft,
thrust the screaming wretch suddenly forward on the
weapon, driving it hilt-deep in his writhing body,
fouling the blade. Before Kane could wrench it clear,
with a yell of triumph the pack rushed in on him and
bore him down by sheer weight of numbers. As they
grappled him from all sides, the Puritan wished in
vain for the dirk he had thrown away. But even so,
his taking was none too easy.

Blood spattered and faces caved in beneath his
iron-hard fists that splintered teeth and shattered bone.
A warrior reeled away disabled from a vicious drive
of knee to groin. Even when they had him stretched

out and piled man-weight on him until he could no longer strike with fists or foot, his long lean fingers sank fiercely through a matted beard to lock about a corded throat in a grip that took the power of three strong men to break and left the victim gasping and green-faced.

At last, panting from the terrific struggle, they had him bound hand and foot and the sheikh, thrusting his pistols back into his silken sash, came striding to stand and look down at his captive. Kane glared up at the tall, lean frame, at the hawk-like face with its black-curled beard and arrogant brown eyes.

"I am the sheikh Hassim ben Said," said the Arab. "Who are you?"

"My name is Solomon Kane," growled the Puritan in the sheikh's own language. "I am an Englishman, you heathen jackal."

The dark eyes of the Arab flickered with interest.

"Suleiman Kahani," said he, giving the Arabesque equivalent of the English name. "I have heard of you—you have fought the Turks betimes and the Barbary corsairs have licked their wounds because of you."

Kane deigned no reply. Hassim shrugged his shoulders.

"You will bring a fine price," said he. "Mayhap I will take you to Stamboul, where there are shas who would desire such a man among their slaves. And I mind me now of one Kemal Bey, a man of ships, who wears a deep scar across his face of your making and who curses the name of Englishman. He will pay me a high price for you. And behold, oh Frank, I do you the honor of appointing you a separate guard. You shall not walk in the yoke-chain but free save for your hands."

Kane made no answer, and at a sign from the sheikh, he was hauled to his feet and his bonds loosened except for his hands, which they left bound firmly behind him. A stout cord was looped about his neck and the other end of this was given into the hand of a huge warrior who bore in his free hand a great curved simitar.

"And now what think ye of my favor to you, Frank?" queried the sheikh.

"I am thinking," answered Kane in a slow, deep voice of menace, "that I would trade my soul's salvation to face you and your sword, alone and unarmed, and to tear the heart from your breast with my naked fingers."

Such was the concentrated hate in his deep resounding voice, and such primal, unconquerable fury blazed from his terrible eyes, that the hardened and fearless chieftain blanched and involuntarily recoiled as if from a maddened beast.

Then Hassim recovered his poise and with a short word to his followers, strode to the head of the cavalcade. Kane noted with thankfulness that the respite occasioned by his capture had given the girl who had fallen a chance to rest and revive. The skinning knife had not had time to more than touch her; she was able to reel along. Night was not far away. Soon the slavers would be forced to halt and camp.

The Englishman perforce took up the trek, his guard remaining a few paces behind with a huge blade ever ready. Kane also noted with a touch of grim vanity, that three more warriors marched close behind, muskets ready and matches burning. They had tasted his prowess and they were taking no chances. His weapons had been recovered and Hassim had promptly appropriated all except the cat-headed ju-ju staff. This had been contemptuously cast aside by him and taken up by one of the savage warriors.

The Englishman was presently aware that a lean, gray-bearded Arab was walking along at his side. This Arab seemed desirous of speaking but strangely timid, and the source of his timidity seemed, curiously enough, the ju-ju stave which he had taken from the man who had picked it up, and which he now turned uncertainly in his hands.

"I am Yussef the Hadji," said this Arab suddenly. "I have naught against you. I had no hand in attacking you and would be your friend if you would let me. Tell me, Frank, whence comes this staff and how comes it into your hands?"

Kane's first inclination was to consign his questioner to the infernal regions, but a certain sincerity of manner in the old man made him change his mind and he answered: "It was given me by my blood-brother—a magician of the Slave Coast, named N'Longa."

The old Arab nodded and muttered in his beard and presently sent a warrior running forward to bid Hassim return. The tall sheikh presently came striding back along the slow-moving column, with a clank and jingle of daggers and sabers, with Kane's dirk and pistols thrust into his wide sash.

"Look, Hassim," the old Arab thrust forward the stave, "you cast it away without knowing what you did!"

"And what of it?" growled the sheikh. "I see naught but a staff—sharp-pointed and with the head of a cat on the other end—a staff with strange infidel carvings upon it."

The older man shook it at him in excitement: "This staff is older than the world! It holds mighty magic! I have read of it in the old iron-bound books and Mohammed—on whom peace!—himself hath spoken of it by allegory and parable! See the cat-head upon it? It is the head of a goddess of ancient Egypt! Ages ago, before Mohammed taught, before Jerusalem was, the priests of Bast bore this rod before the bowing, chanting worshippers! With it Musa did wonders before Pharaoh and when the Yahudi fled from Egypt they bore it with them. And for centuries it was the scepter of Israel and Judah and with it Sulieman ben Daoud drove forth the conjurers and magicians and prisoned the efreets and the evil genii! Look! Again in the hands of a Sulieman we find the ancient rod!"

Old Yussef had worked himself into a pitch of almost fanatic fervor but Hassim merely shrugged his shoulders.

"It did not save the Jews from bondage nor this Sulieman from our captivity," said he. "I value it not as much as I esteem the long thin blade with which he loosed the souls of three of my best swordsmen."

Yussef shook his head. "Your mockery will bring you to no good end, Hassim. Some day you will meet a power that will not divide before your sword or fall to your bullets. I will keep the staff, and I warn you—abuse not the Frank. He has borne the holy and terrible staff of Sulieman and Musa and the Pharaohs, and who knows what magic he has drawn therefrom? For it is older than the world and has known the terrible hands of strange pre-Adamite priests in the silent cities beneath the seas, and has drawn from an Elder World mystery and magic unguessed by humankind. There were strange kings and stranger priests when the dawns were young, and evil was, even in their day. And with this staff they fought the evil which was ancient when their strange world was young, so many millions of years ago that a man would shudder to count them."

Hassim answered impatiently and strode away with old Yussef following him persistently and chattering away in a querulous tone. Kane shrugged his mighty shoulders. With what he knew of the strange powers of that strange staff, he was not one to question the old man's assertions, fantastic as they seemed.

This much he knew—that it was made of a wood that existed nowhere on earth today. It needed but the proof of sight and touch to realize that its material had grown in some world apart. The exquisite workmanship of the head, of a pre-pyramidal age, and the hieroglyphics, symbols of a language that was forgotten when Rome was young—these, Kane sensed, were additions as modern to the antiquity of the staff itself as would be English words carved on the stone monoliths of Stonehenge.

As for the cat-head—looking at it sometimes Kane had a peculiar feeling of alteration; a faint sensing that once the pommel of the staff was carved with a different design. The dust-ancient Egyptian who had carved the head of Bast had merely altered the original figure, and what that figure had been, Kane had never tried to guess. A close scrutiny of the staff always aroused a disquieting and almost dizzy suggestion of abysses of eons, unprovocative to further speculation.

The day wore on. The sun beat down mercilessly, then screened itself in the great trees as it slanted toward the horizon. The slaves suffered fiercely for water and a continual whimpering rose from their ranks as they staggered blindly on. Some fell and half-crawled, and were half-dragged by their reeling yoke-mates. When all were buckling from exhaustion, the sun dipped, night rushed on, and a halt was called. Camp was pitched, guards thrown out. The slaves were fed scantily and given enough water to keep life in them—but only just enough. Their fetters were not loosened, but they were allowed to sprawl about as they might. Their fearful thirst and hunger having been somewhat eased, they bore the discomforts of their shackles with characteristic stoicism.

Kane was fed without his hands being untied, and he was given all the water he wished. The patient eyes of the slaves watched him drink, silently, and he was sorely ashamed to guzzle what others suffered for; he ceased before his thirst was fully quenched. A wide clearing had been selected, on all sides of which rose gigantic trees. After the Arabs had eaten and while the black Moslems were still cooking their food, old Yussef came to Kane and began to talk about the staff again. Kane answered his questions with admirable patience, considering the hatred he bore the whole race to which the Hadji belonged, and during the conversation, Hassim came striding up and looked down in contempt. Hassim, Kane ruminated, was the very symbol of militant Islam—bold, reckless, materialistic, sparing nothing, fearing nothing, as sure of his own destiny and as contemptuous of the rights of others as the most powerful Western king.

"Are you maundering about that stick again?" he gibed. "Hadji, you grow childish in your old age."

Yussef's beard quivered in anger. He shook the staff at his sheikh like a threat of evil.

"Your mockery little befits your rank, Hassim," he snapped. "We are in the heart of a dark and demon-haunted land, to which long ago were banished the devils from Arabia. If this staff, which any but a fool can tell is no rod of any world we know, has existed down to our day, who knows what other things, tangible or intangible, may have existed through the ages? This very trail we follow—know you how old it is? Men followed it before the Seljuk came out of the East or the Roman came out of the West. Over this very trail, legends say, the great Sulieman came when he drove the demons westward out of Asia and prisoned them in strange prisons. And will you say—"

A wild shout interrupted him. Out of the shadows of the jungle a warrior came flying as if from the hounds of Doom. With arms flinging wildly, eyes rolling to display the whites, and mouth wide open so that all his gleaming teeth were visible, he made an image of stark terror not soon forgotten. The Moslem horde leaped up, snatching their weapons, and Hassim swore: "That's Ali, whom I sent to scout for meat—perchance a lion—"

But no lion followed the man who fell at Hassim's feet, mouthing gibberish and pointing wildly back at the black jungle whence the nerve-strung watchers expected some brain-shattering horror to burst.

"He says he found a strange mausoleum back in the jungle," said Hassim with a scowl, "but he cannot tell what frightened him. He only knows a great horror overwhelmed him and sent him flying. Ali, you are a fool and a rogue."

He kicked the groveling savage viciously, but the

other Arabs drew about him in some uncertainty. The panic was spreading among the native warriors.

"They will bolt in spite of us," muttered a bearded Arab, uneasily watching the native allies who milled together, jabbered excitedly and flung fearsome glances over the shoulders. "Hassim, 'twere better to march on a few miles. This is an evil place after all, and though 'tis likely the fool, Ali, was frightened by his own shadow—still—"

"Still," jeered the sheikh, "you will all feel better when we have left it behind. Good enough; to still your fears I will move camp—but first I will have a look at this thing. Lash up the slaves; we'll swing into the jungle and pass by this mausoleum; perhaps some great king lies there. No one will be afraid if we all go in a body with guns."

So the weary slaves were whipped into wakefulness and stumbled along beneath the whips again. The native allies went silently and nervously, reluctantly obeying Hassim's implacable will but huddling close to the Arabs. The moon had risen, huge, red and sullen, and the jungle was bathed in a sinister silver glow that etched the brooding trees in black shadow. The trembling Ali pointed out the way, somewhat reassured by his savage master's presence.

And so they passed through the jungle until they came to a strange clearing among the giant trees—strange because nothing grew there. The trees ringed it in a disquieting symmetrical manner, and no lichen or moss grew on the earth, which seemed to have been blasted and blighted in a strange fashion. And in the midst of the glade stood the mausoleum.

A great brooding mass of stone it was, pregnant with ancient evil. Dead with the dead of a hundred centuries it seemed, yet Kane was aware that the air pulsed about it, as with the slow, unhuman breathing of some gigantic, invisible monster.

The Arabs' native allies drew back muttering, assailed by the evil atmosphere of the place. The slaves stood in a patient, silent group beneath the trees. The Arabs went forward to the frowning black mass, and Yussef, taking Kane's cord from his guard, led the Englishman with him like a surly mastiff, as if for protection against the unknown.

"Some mighty sultan doubtless lies here," said Hassim, tapping the stone with his scabbard.

"Whence come these stones?" muttered Yussef uneasily. "They are of dark and forbidding aspect. Why should a great sultan lie in state so far from any habitation of man? If there were ruins of an old city hereabouts it would be different—"

He bent to examine the heavy metal door with its huge lock, curiously sealed and fused. He shook his head forebodingly as he made out the ancient Hebraic characters carved on the door.

"I can not read them," he quavered, "and belike it is well for me I can not. What ancient kings sealed up is not good for men to disturb. Hassim, let us hence. This place is pregnant with evil for the sons of men."

But Hassim gave him no heed. "He who lies within is no son of Islam," said he, "and why should we not despoil him of the gems and riches that undoubtedly were laid to rest with him? Let us break open this door."

Some of the Arabs shook their heads doubtfully but Hassim's word was law. Calling to him a huge warrior who bore a heavy hammer, he ordered him to break open the door.

As the man swung up his sledge, Kane gave a sharp exclamation. Was he mad? The apparent antiquity of this brooding mass of stone was proof that it had stood undisturbed for thousands of years. Yet he could have sworn that he heard the sounds of footfalls within! Back and forth they padded, as if something paced the narrow confines of that grisly prison in a never-ending monotony of movement.

A cold hand touched the spine of Solomon Kane. Whether the sounds registered on his conscious ear or on some unsounded deep of soul or sub-feeling, he could not tell, but he knew that somewhere within his consciousness there re-echoed the tramp of monstrous feet from within that ghastly mausoleum.

"Stop!" he exclaimed. "Hassim, I may be mad, but I hear the tread of some fiend within that pile of stone."

Hassim raised his hand and checked the hovering hammer. He listened intently, and the others strained their ears in a silence that had suddenly become tense.

"I hear nothing," grunted a bearded giant.

"Nor I," came a quick chorus. "The Frank is mad!"

"Hear ye anything, Yussef?" asked Hassim sardonically.

The old Hadji shifted nervously. His face was uneasy.

"No, Hassim, no, yet—"

Kane decided he must be mad. Yet in his heart he knew he was never saner, and he knew somehow that this occult keenness of the deeper senses that set him apart from the Arabs came from long association with the ju-ju staff that old Yussef now held in his shaking hands.

Hassim laughed harshly and made a gesture to the warrior. The hammer fell with a crash that re-echoed deafeningly and shivered off through the black jungle in a strangely altered cachinnation. Again—again— and again the hammer fell, driven with all the power of rippling muscles and mighty body. And between the blows Kane still heard that lumbering tread, and he who had never known fear as men know it, felt the cold hand of terror clutching at his heart.

This fear was apart from earthly or mortal fear, as the sound of the footfalls was apart from mortal tread. Kane's fright was like a cold wind blowing on him from outer realms of unguessed Darkness, bearing him the evil and decay of an outlived epoch and an unutterably ancient period. Kane was not sure whether he heard those footfalls or by some dim instinct sensed them. But he was sure of their reality.

They were not the tramp of man or beast; but inside that black, hideously ancient mausoleum some nameless thing moved with soul-shaking and elephantine tread.

The powerful warrior seated and panted with the difficulty of his task. But at last, beneath the heavy blows the ancient lock shattered; the hinges snapped; the door burst inward. And Yussef screamed.

From that black gaping entrance no tiger-fanged beast or demon of solid flesh and blood leaped forth. But a fearful stench flowed out in billowing, almost tangible waves and in one brain-shattering, ravening rush, whereby the gaping door seemed to gush blood, the Horror was upon them. It enveloped Hassim, and the fearless chieftain, hewing vainly at the almost intangible terror, screamed with sudden, unaccustomed fright as his lashing simitar whistled only through stuff as yielding and unharmable as air, and he felt himself lapped by coils of death and destruction.

Yussef shrieked like a lost soul, dropped the ju-ju stave and joined his fellows who streamed out into the jungle in mad flight, preceded by their howling allies. Only the slaves fled not, but stood shackled to their doom, wailing their terror. As in a nightmare of delirium Kane saw Hassim swaying like a reed in the wind, lapped about by a gigantic pulsing red Thing that had neither shape nor earthly substance. Then, as the crack of splintering bones came to him, and the sheikh's body buckled like a straw beneath a stamping hoof, the Englishman burst his bonds with one volcanic effort and caught up the ju-ju stave.

Hassim was down, crushed and dead, sprawled like a broken toy with shattered limbs awry, and the red pulsing Thing was lurching toward Kane like a thick cloud of blood in the air, that continually changed its shape and form, and yet somehow trod lumberingly as if on monstrous legs!

Kane felt the cold fingers of fear claw at his brain, but he braced himself, and lifting the ancient staff, struck with all his power into the center of the Horror. And he felt an unnamable, immaterial substance meet and give way before the falling staff. Then he was almost strangled by the nauseous burst of unholy stench that flooded the air, and somewhere down the dim vistas of his soul's consciousness re-echoed unbearably a hideous formless cataclysm that he knew was the death-screaming of the monster. For it was down and dying at his feet, its crimson paling in slow surges like the rise and receding of red waves on some foul coast. And as it paled, the soundless screaming dwindled away into cosmic distances as though it faded into some sphere apart and aloof beyond human ken.

Kane, dazed and incredulous, looked down on a shapeless, colorless, all but invisible mass at his feet which he knew was the corpse of the Horror, dashed back into the black realms from whence it had come, by a single blow of the staff of Solomon. Aye, the same staff, Kane knew, that in the hands of a mighty king and magician had ages ago driven the monster into that strange prison, to bide until ignorant hands loosed it again upon the world.

The old tales were true then, and King Solomon had in truth driven the demons westward and sealed them in strange places. Why had he let them live? Was human magic too weak in those dim days to more than subdue the devils? Kane shrugged his shoulders in wonderment. He knew nothing of magic, yet he had slain where that other Solomon had but imprisoned.

And Solomon Kane shuddered, for he had looked on Life that was not Life as he knew it, and had dealt and witnessed Death that was not Death as he knew it. Again the realization swept over him, as it had in the dust-haunted halls of Atlantean Negari, as it had in the abhorrent Hills of the Dead, as it had in Akaana—that human life was but one of a myriad forms of existence, that worlds existed within worlds, and that there was more than one plane of existence.

The planet men call the earth spun on through the untold ages, Kane realized, and as it spun it spawned Life, and living things which wriggled about it as maggots are spawned in rot and corruption. Man was the dominant maggot now—why should he in his pride suppose that he and his adjuncts were the first maggots—or the last to rule a planet quick with unguessed life.

He shook his head, gazing in new wonder at the ancient gift of N'Longa, seeing in it at last not merely a tool of black magic, but a sword of good and light against the powers of inhuman evil forever. And he was shaken with a strange reverence for it that was almost fear.

Then he bent to the Thing at his feet, shuddering to feel its strange mass slip through his fingers like wisps of heavy fog. He thrust the staff beneath it and somehow lifted and levered the mass back into the mausoleum and shut the door.

Then he stood gazing down at the strangely mutilated body of Hassim, noting how it was smeared with foul slime and how it had already begun to decompose. He shuddered again, and suddenly a low timid voice aroused him from his sombre cogitations. The captives knelt beneath the trees and watched with great patient eyes. With a start he shook off his strange mood. He took from the moldering corpse his own pistols, dirk and rapier, making shift to wipe off the clinging foulness that was already flecking the steel with rust. He also took up a quantity of powder and shot dropped by the Arabs in their frantic flight. He knew they would return no more. They might die in their flight, or they might gain through the interminable leagues of jungle to the coast; but they would not turn back to dare the terror of that grisly glade.

Kane came to the wretched slaves and after some difficulty released them.

"Take up these weapons which the warriors dropped in their haste," said he, "and get you home. This is an evil place. Get ye back to your villages and when the next Arabs come, die in the ruins of your huts rather than be slaves."

Then they would have knelt and kissed his feet, but he, in much confusion, forebade them roughly. Then as they made preparations to go, one said to him: "Master, what of thee? Wilt thou not return with us? Thou shalt be our king!"

But Kane shook his head.

"I go eastward," said he. And so the tribes-people bowed to him and turned back on the long trail to their own homeland. And Kane shouldered the staff that had been the rod of the Pharaohs and of Moses and of Solomon and of nameless Atlantean kings behind them, and turned his face eastward, halting only for a single backward glance at the great mausoleum that other Solomon had built with strange arts so long ago, and which now loomed dark and forever silent against the stars.

THE CHILDREN OF ASSHUR*

I

Solomon Kane started up in the darkness, snatching at the weapons which lay on the pile of skins that served him as a crude pallet. It was not the mad drum of the tropic rain on the leaves of the hut roof which had wakened him, nor the bellowing of the thunder. It was the screams of human agony, the clash of steel that cut through the din of the tropical storm. Some sort of a conflict was taking place in the native village in which he had sought refuge from the storm, and it sounded much like a raid in force. As Solomon groped for his sword, he wondered what bushmen would raid a village in the night and in such a storm as this. His pistols lay beside his sword, but he did not take them up, knowing that they would be useless in such a torrent of rain—a rain which would wet their priming instantly.

He had laid down fully clad, save for his slouch hat and cloak, and without stopping for them, he ran to the door of the hut. A ragged streak of lightning which seemed to rip the sky open showed him a chaotic glimpse of struggling figures in the spaces between the huts, dazzlingly glinting back from flashing steel. Above the storm he heard the shrieks of the black people and deep-toned shouts in a language unfamiliar to him. Springing from the hut he sensed the presence of one in front of him; then another thun-

---
* Completed by J. Ramsey Campbell.

derous burst of fire ripped across the sky, limning all in a weird blue light. In that flashing instant Solomon thrust savagely, felt the blade bend double in his hand, and saw a heavy sword swinging for his head. A burst of sparks, brighter than the lightning, exploded before his eyes; then blackness darker than the jungle night engulfed him.

Dawn was spreading pallidly over the dripping jungle reaches when Solomon Kane stirred and sat up in the ooze before the hut. Blood had caked on his scalp and his head ached slightly. Shaking off a slight grogginess, he rose. The rain had long since ceased, the skies were clear. Silence lay over the village, and Kane saw that it was in truth a village of the dead. Corpses of men, women, and children lay strewn everywhere—in the streets, in the doorways of the huts, inside the huts, some of which had been literally ripped to pieces, either in search of cowering victims, or in sheer wantoness of destruction. They had not taken many prisoners, Solomon decided, whoever the unknown raiders might be. Nor had they taken the spears, axes, cooking pots, and plumed head-pieces of their victims, this fact seeming to argue a raid by a race superior in culture and artizanship to the crude villagers. But they had taken all the ivory they could find, and they had taken, Kane discovered, his rapier and his dirk, pistols, and powder-and-shot pouches. And they had taken his staff, the sharp-pointed, strangely-carved, cat-headed stave, which his friend, N'Longa, the West Coast witch-man, had given him, as well as his hat and cloak.

Kane stood in the center of the desolated village, brooding over the matter, strange speculations running at random through his mind. His conversation with the natives of the village, into which he had made his way the night before out of the storm-beaten jungle, gave him no clue as to the nature of the raiders. The natives themselves had known little about the land into which they had but recently come, driven over a long trek by a rival, more powerful tribe. They had been a simple, good-natured people, who had welcomed him into their huts and given him freely of their humble goods. Kane's heart was hot with wrath against their unknown destroyers, but even deeper than that burned his unquenchable curiosity, the curse of the intelligent man.

For Kane had looked on mystery in the night. And the storm—that vivid flame of lightning—had showed him etched momentarily in its glare a fierce, black-bearded race—the face of a white man. Yet according to sanity there could be no white men—not even Arab raiders—within hundreds and hundreds of miles. Kane had had no time to observe the man's dress, but he had a vague impression that the figure was clad bizarrely. And that sword which, striking glancing and flat, had struck him down—surely that had been no crude native weapon.

Kane glanced at the crude mud wall which surrounded the village, at the bamboo gates which now lay in ruins—hewn to pieces by the raiders. The storm had apparently abated when the raiders marched forth, for he made out a broad trampled track leading out of the broken gate and into the jungle.

Kane picked up a crude native ax that lay nearby. If any of the unknown slayers had fallen in the battle, their bodies had been carried away by their companions. Leaves pieced together made him a makeshift hat to protect his head from the force of the sun. Then Solomon Kane went through the broken gate and into the dripping jungle, following the spoor of the unknown.

Under the giant trees the tracks became clearer, and Kane made out that most of them were of sandals —a type of sandal, likewise, that was strange to him. The remaining tracks were of bare feet, indicating that some prisoners had been taken. Apparently they had a long start for, though he travelled without pause, swinging along tirelessly on his rangy legs, he did not sight the column in that day's march.

He ate of the food he had brought from the ruined village, and pressed on without halting, consumed by anger and with the desire to solve the mystery of that lightning-limned face; more, the raiders had taken his weapons, and in that dark land a man's weapons were his life. The day wore on. As the sun sank, the jungle gave way to forest-land, and at twilight Kane came out on a rolling, grass-grown, tree-dotted plain, and saw far across it what appeared to be a low-lying range of hills. The tracks led straight out across the plain, and Kane believed the raiders' goal was those low, even hills.

He hesitated; across the grasslands came the thunderous roaring of lions, echoing and re-echoing from a score of different points. The great cats were beginning to stalk their prey, and it would be suicide to venture across that vast open space, armed with only an ax. Kane found a giant tree and, clambering into it, settled himself in a crotch as comfortably as he might. Far out across the plain he saw a point of light twinkling among the hills. Then on the plain, approaching the hills, he saw other lights, a twinkling fire-set serpentine line that moved toward the hills, now scarcely visible against the stars along the horizon. It was the column of raiders with their captives, he realized. They were bearing torches and travelling swiftly. The torches were no doubt to keep off the lions, and Kane decided that their goal must be very near at hand if they risked a night march on those carnivora-haunted grasslands.

As he watched, he saw the twinkling fire-points move upward, and for awhile they glittered among the hills; then he saw them no more.

Speculating on the mystery of it all, Kane slept, while the night winds whispered dark secrets of ancient Africa among the leaves, and lions roared beneath his tree, lashing their tufted tails as they gazed upward with hungry eyes.

Again dawn lighted the land with rose and gold, and Solomon descended from his perch and took up his journey. He ate the last of the food he had brought, drank from a stream that looked fairly pure, and speculated on the chance of finding food among the hills. If he did not find it, he might be in a precarious position, but Kane had been hungry before— aye, and starving and freezing and weary. His rangy, broad-shouldered frame was hard as iron, pliant as steel.

So he swung boldly out across the savannas, watching warily for lurking lions, but slackening not his pace. The sun climbed to the zenith and dipped westward. As he approached the low range, it began to grow in distinctness. He saw that instead of rugged hills, he was approaching a low plateau that rose abruptly from the surrounding plain and appeared to be level. He saw trees and tall grass on the edges, but the cliffs seemed barren and rough. However, they were at no point more than seventy or eighty feet in height, as far as he could see, and he anticipated no great difficulty in surmounting them.

Approaching them he saw that they were almost solid rock, though overlaid by a fairly thick stratum of soil. Boulders had tumbled down in many places and he saw that an active man could scale the cliffs in many places. But he saw something else—a broad road which wound up the steep pitch of the precipice, and up which led the spoors he was following.

Kane approached the road, noting the excellence of the road's workmanship—certainly no mere animal path or even a native trail. The road had been cut into the cliff with consummate skill, and it was paved and palustraded with smoothly cut blocks of stone.

Wary as a wolf, he avoided the road; further on he found a less steep slope up which he went. It was unstable footing, and boulders that seemed to poise on the slope threatened to roll down upon him, but he accomplished the task without undue hazard and came out over the edge of the cliff.

Kane stood on a rugged, boulder-strewn slope, which pitched off rather steeply onto a flat expanse. From where he stood, he saw the broad plateau spread out beneath his feet, carpeted with lush green grass. And in the midst—he blinked his eyes and shook his head, thinking he looked on some mirage or hallucination. No! It was still there: a massive walled city, rearing from the grassy plain. He saw the battlements, the towers beyond, with small figures moving about them. On the other side of the city he made out a small lake, on the shores of which stretched luxuriant gardens and fields, and meadow-like expanses filled with grazing cattle.

Amazement at the sight held the Puritan frozen for an instant; then the clink of an iron heel on a stone brought him quickly about to face the man who had come from among the boulders. This man was broad-built and powerful, almost as tall as Kane, and heavier. His bare arms bulged with muscles, and his legs were like knotted iron pillars. His face was a duplicate of that Kane had seen in the lightning flash—fierce black-bearded; the face of a white man with arrogant eyes and a predatory hooked nose. From his bull-throat to his knees he was clad in a corselet of iron scales, and on his head was an iron helmet. A metal-braced shield of hardwood and leather was on his left arm, a dagger in his girdle, and a short but heavy iron mace in his hand.

All this Kane saw in a glance as the man roared and leaped. The Englishman realized in that instant that there was to be no such thing as a parley. It was to be a battle to the death. As a tiger leaps, he sprang to meet the warrior, launching his ax with all the power of that rangy frame. The warrior caught the blow in his shield. The ax-edge turned, the haft splintering in Kane's hand, the buckler shattered.

Carried by the momentum of his savage lunge, Kane's body crashed against his foe who dropped the useless shield and, staggering, grappled with the Englishman. Straining and gasping they reeled on hard-braced feet, and Kane snarled like a wolf as he felt the full power of his foe's strength. The armor hampered the Englishman, and the warrior had shortened his grasp on the iron mace and was ferociously striving to crash it on Kane's bare head.

The Englishman was striving to pinion the warrior's arm, but his clutching fingers missed, and the mace crashed sickeningly against his bare head. Again it fell, as a fire-shot mist clouded Kane's vision, but his instinctive wrench avoided it, though it halfnumbed his shoulder, ripping the skin so that the blood started in streams.

Maddened, Kane lunged fiercely against the stalwart body of the mace-wielder, and one blindly grasping hand closed on the dagger hilt at the warrior's girdle. Ripping it forth, he stabbed blindly and savagely.

Close-locked, the fighters staggered backward, the one stabbing in venomous silence, the other striving to tear his arm free so that he might crash home one destroying blow. The warrior's short, half-hindered blows glanced from Kane's head and shoulders, lacerating the skin and bringing blood in streams. Red lances of agony pierced the Englishman's clouding brain. And still the dagger in his lunging hand glanced from the iron scales that guarded his foe's body.

Blinded, dazed, fighting on instinct alone as a wounded wolf fights, Kane's teeth snapped, fang-like, into the great bull throat of his foe. The torn flesh and a burst of flooding blood brought an agonized roar from the powerful frame. The lashing mace faltered and the warrior flinched back. They reeled on the edge of a low precipice and pitched, rolling headlong and close clinched. At the foot of the slope they brought up, Kane uppermost. The dagger in his hand glittered high above his head and flashed downward, sinking hilt-deep in the warrior's throat. Kane's body pitched forward with the blow and he lay senseless above his slain enemy.

They lay in a widening pool of blood. In the sky specks appeared, black against the blue, wheeling, circling, and dropping lower.

Then from among the defiles appeared men similar in apparel and appearance to he who lay dead beneath Kane's senseless body. They had been attracted by the sounds of battle, and now they stood about discussing the matter in harsh and gutteral tones. Slaves stood a little way from them in complete silence.

They dragged the forms apart and discovered that one was dead, one probably dying. Then, after some discussion, they made a litter of their spears and sword-slings, and ordered their slaves to lift the bodies and carry them. The party set out toward the city which gleamed strangely in the midst of the grassy plain.

II

Consciousness returned to Solomon Kane. He was lying on a couch covered with finely dressed skins and furs, in a large chamber, whose floor, walls, and ceiling were of stone. There was one window, heavily barred, and a single doorway. Outside stood a stalwart warrior, in appearance much like the man he had slain.

Then Kane discovered another thing; golden chains were on his wrists, neck, and ankles. They were linked together in an intricate pattern, and were made fast to a ring set in the wall with a strong silver lock.

Kane found that his wounds had been bandaged, and as he pondered over his situation a slave entered with food and a kind of purple wine. The Englishman made no attempt at conversation, but ate the food offered and drank deeply. The wine was drugged, and he soon fell asleep. Many hours later when he awakened, he found that the bandages had been changed. A different guard stood outside the door—a man of the same cast as the former soldier, however—muscular, black-bearded, and clad in armor.

This time when he awakened he felt strong and refreshed. Kane quickly decided that when the slave returned he would seek to learn something of the curious environs into which he had fallen. The scruff of leather sandals on the tilings announced the approach of someone, and Kane sat up on his couch as a group of figures entered the chamber.

In the background lurked the slave who had brought Kane's food. Before him, a group of men had assembled in a little clump; robed, inscrutable, shaven of face and head. And a little apart from them stood a man whose figure dominated the whole scene. He was tall, with garments of silk bound by a golden-scaled girdle. His blue-black hair and beard were curiously curled; his hawk-nosed face cruel and predatory. The arrogance of the eyes, which Kane had noticed as characteristic of the unknown race, was in this man much more evident than in the others. On his head was a curiously carved circlet of gold, in his hand a golden wand. The attitude of the rest toward him was one of cringing servility, and Kane believed that he looked upon either the king or the high priest of the city.

Beside this personage stood a shorter, fatter man, with shaven face and head, clad in robes much like those worn by the lesser persons in the background, but far more costly. In his hand he bore a scourge composed of six thongs made fast to a jewel-set handle. The thongs ended in triangular shaped bits of metal, and the whole represented as savage an implement of punishment as Kane had ever looked upon. The man who bore this had small eyes, shifty and crafty, and his whole attitude was a mixture of fawning servility toward the man with the sceptre, and of intolerant despotism toward the lesser beings.

Kane gave back their stare, trying to place an elusive sense of familiarity. There was something in the features of these people which vaguely suggested the Arab; yet they were strangely unlike any Arabs he had ever seen. They spoke together, and their language at times had a somehow familiar sound. But he could not define these faint stirrings of half-memory.

At last the tall man with the scepter turned and strode majestically forth, followed by his slavish companions. Kane was left alone. After a time the fat second in command returned with half a dozen soldiers and acolytes. Among these was the young slave who brought Kane's food, and a tall and sombre figure, naked but for a loin cloth, who bore a great key at his girdle. The soldiers ringed Kane, javelins ready, while this man unlocked the chains from the ring in the wall. They surrounded him and, holding to his chains, indicated that he was to march with them. Surrounded by his captors, Kane emerged from the chamber into what appeared to be a series of wide galleries winding about the interior of the vast structure. Tier by tier they mounted and turned at last into a chamber much like that he had left, similarly furnished. Kane's chains were made fast to a ring in the stone wall near the single window. He could stand upright, or lie, or sit on the skin-piled couch, but he could not move half a dozen steps in any direction. Wine and food were placed at his disposal.

His captors left him, and Kane noticed that neither was the door bolted nor a guard placed before it. He decided that they considered his chains sufficient to keep him safe, and after testing them he realized that they were right. Yet, there was another reason for their apparent carelessness, as he was to learn.

The Englishman looked out of the window, which was larger than the other had been and not so thickly barred. He was looking out over the city from a considerable height. Below him were narrow streets, broad avenues flanked by what seemed to be columns and carven stone lions, and on wide expanses of flat-roofed houses. Many of the buildings were of stone, and others were of a sun-dried brick. There was a massiveness about this architecture that was vaguely repellent—a sombre, heavy motif that seemed to suggest a sullen and slightly inhuman character of the builders.

A wall that surrounded the city was tall and thick, with towers spaced at regular intervals. He saw armored figures moving sentinel-like along the wall, and meditated upon the warlike aspect of this people. The streets and market places below him offered a colorful maze as the richly clad people moved in an ever-shifting panorama.

As for the building which was his prison, Kane could make out little of its nature. Yet, below him he saw a series of massive tiers descending like giant stair-steps. It must be, he decided with a rather unpleasant sensation, built much like the fabled Tower of Babel, one tier above another.

Kane turned his attention back to his chamber. The walls were rich in mural decorations, carvings painted in various colors, well-tinted and blended. Indeed, the art was of as high a standard as any the Englishman had ever seen in Asia or in Europe. Most of the scenes were of war or of the hunt—powerful men with black beards that were often curled, in armor, slaying lions and driving other warriors before them. Some of the pursued warriors were naked black men; others closely resembled their pursuers.

The human figures were not as well depicted as those of the beasts; they were conventionalized to a point that often lent them a somewhat wooden aspect. But the lions were portrayed with vivid realism. Some of the scenes showed the black-bearded slayers in chariots, drawn by fire-breathing steeds, and Kane felt again that strange sense of familiarity, as if he had seen these scenes—or similar scenes—before. The chariots and horses, he noted, were inferior in life-likeness to the lions. The fault was not in conventionalization but in the artist's ignorance of his subject,

Kane decided, noting mistakes that seemed incongruous considering the skill with which they were portrayed.

Time passed swiftly as he pondered over the carvings. Presently the silent slave entered with food and wine.

When he set down the viands, Kane spoke to him in a dialect of the bush tribes, to one of the divisions of which he believed the man belonged, having noted certain tribal scars on his features. The dull face lighted slightly, and the man answered in a tongue similar enough for Kane to understand him.

"What city is this?"

"Ninn, bwana."

"Who are these people?"

The dull slave shook his head in doubt.

"They be very old people, bwana. They have dwelt here very long time."

"Was that their king who came to my chamber with his men?"

"Yes, bwana. That be King Asshur-ras-arab."

"And the man with the lash?"

"Yamen, the priest, bwana Persian."

"Why do you call me that?" asked Kane nonplussed.

"So the masters name you, bwana—" the slave shrank back and his skin turned ashy as the shadow of a tall figure fell across the doorway. A shaven-headed, half-naked giant entered, and the slave fell to his knees wailing his terror. Mighty fingers closed about the terrified throat, and Kane saw the wretched slave's eyes protruding, his tongue thrust from his gaping mouth. His body writhed and threshed unavailingly; hands clawed weakly and more weakly at iron wrists. Then he went limp in his slayer's hands. As the shaven-headed warrior released him, the corpse slumped loosely to the floor. The warrior smote his hands together, and a pair of slaves entered. Their faces turned ashy at the sight of their companion's corpse, but at a gesture they callously laid hold of the dead man's feet and dragged him forth.

The warrior turned at the door and his opaque and implacable eyes met Kane's gaze, as if in warning. Hate drummed in Kane's temples, and it was the grim eyes of the murderer which fell before the cold fury in the Englishman's glare. The man went noiselessly forth, leaving Kane to his meditations.

When food was next brought to Kane, it was carried by a rangy young slave of genial and intelligent appearance. Kane made no effort to speak to him; apparently the masters did not wish for their captive to learn anything about them for some reason or another.

How many days Kane remained in the high-flung chamber, he did not know. Each day was exactly like the last, and he lost count of time. Sometimes Yamen the priest came and looked upon him with a satisfied air that made Kane's eyes turn red with the killer's lust; sometimes the giant murderer noiselessly appeared, to disappear just as noiselessly.

Kane's eyes were riveted to the key that swung from the silent giant's girdle. Could he but once get within reach of the fellow—but his captor was careful to stay out of reach unless Kane was surrounded by warriors with readied javelins.

Then one night to his chamber came Yamen the priest with the silent giant who was called Shem and some fifty acolytes and soldiers. It was Shem who unlocked Kane's chains from the wall, and, between two columns of soldiers and priests, the Englishman was escorted along the winding galleries that were lighted by flaring torches set in the niches along the walls, and borne in the hands of the priests.

By the light Kane again observed the carven figures marching everlastingly around the massive walls of the galleries. Many were life-sized, some dimmed and somewhat defaced as with age. Most of these, Kane noted, portrayed men in chariots drawn by horses, and he decided that the later, imperfect figures

THE CHILDREN OF ASSHUR

of steeds and chariots, had been copied from these older carvings. Apparently there were no horses or chariots in the city now. Various racial distinctions were evident in the human figures—the hooked noses and curled black beards of the dominant race were plainly distinguishable. Their opponents were sometimes black men, sometimes men like themselves, and occasionally tall, rangy men with unmistakable Arab features.

Kane was startled to note that in some of the older scenes, men were depicted whose apparel and figures were entirely different from those of the Ninnites. These strangers were always pictured in battle scenes and, significantly Kane thought, not always in retreat. Frequently they seemed to be having the best of the fight, and nowhere could the Englishman find them portrayed as slaves. But what interested him was the familiarity—those carven features were like the countenance of a friend in a strange land to the wanderer. Apart from their strange, barbaric arms and apparel they might have been Englishmen, with their European features and yellow locks.

Somewhere, in the long, long ago, Kane knew, the ancestors of the men of Ninn had warred with men kin to his own ancestors. But in what age and in what land? Certainly the scenes were not laid in the country that was now the homeland of the Ninnites, for these scenes showed fertile plains, grassy hills, and wide rivers. Aye, and great cities like Ninn, but strangely unlike.

And suddenly Kane remembered where he had seen similar carvings, wherein kings with black curled beards slew lions from chariots. He had seen them on crumbling pieces of masonry that marked the site of a long forgotten city in Mesopotamia, and men had told him those ruins were all that remained of Nineveh the Bloody, the accursed of God.

The Englishman and his captors had reached the ground tier of the great temple, and they passed between huge columns, squat and carven like the walls.

At length they came to a vast circular space between the massive wall and the flanking pillars. Cut from the stone of the mighty wall sat a colossal idol—carven features as devoid of human weakness and kindness as the face of a Stone Age monster.

Facing the idol on a stone throne in the shadow of the pillars sat the King, Asshur-ras-arab. The firelight flickered on his strongly chiseled face so that at first Kane thought it was an idol that sat on the throne.

Before the god and facing the king's throne was another, smaller throne. A brazier on a golden tripod stood before it; coals glowed in the brazier and smoke curled languorously upward.

A flowing robe of shimmering green silk was put upon Kane, hiding his tattered and stained garments and the golden chains. He was motioned to sit in the throne before the brazier, and he did so without a sound. Then his ankles and wrists were locked cunningly to the throne, hidden by the folds of the silken robe.

The lesser priests and the soldiers melted away, leaving only Kane, the priest Yamen, and the king upon his throne. Back in the shadows among the treelike columns Kane occasionally glimpsed a glint of metal like fireflies in the dark. Warriors still lurked there, out of sight. He sensed that some sort of a stage had been set. Kane felt a suggestion of charlatanry in the whole procedure.

Now Asshur-ras-arab lifted the golden wand and struck once upon a gong that hung near his throne. A full and mellow note like a distant chime echoed among the dim reaches of the shadowy temple. Along the dusky avenue between the columns came a group of men whom Kane realized must be the nobles of that fantastic city. They were tall men, black-bearded and haughty of bearing, clad in shimmering silk and gleaming gold. And among them walked one in golden chains, a youth whose attitude seemed a mixture of apprehension and defiance.

The assemblage knelt before the king, bowing their

heads to the floor. At a word from him, they arose and faced the Englishman and the god behind him. Now Yamen, with the firelight glinting on his shaven head and into his evil eyes so that he looked like a paunchy demon, cried out a sort of weird chant and flung a handful of powder into the brazier. Instantly a greenish smoke billowed upward, half-veiling Kane's face. The Englishman gagged; the smell and taste were unpleasant in the extreme. He felt groggy, drugged. His brain reeled like a drunken man's, and he tore savagely at his chains. Only half-conscious of what he said, unaccustomed oaths ripped from his lips.

He was dimly aware that Yamen cried out fiercely at his curses, the priest leaning forward in an attitude of listening. Then the powder burned out, the smoke waned away, and Kane sat groggy and bewildered on the throne.

Yamen turned toward the king and bent low. He straightened and, with his arms outstretched, spoke in a sonorous tone. The king solemnly repeated his words and Kane saw the face of the noble prisoner go white. Then his captors seized his arms, and the band marched slowly away, their footfalls coming back eerily through the shadowy vastness.

Like silent ghosts the soldiers came from the shadows and unchained him. Again they grouped themselves about Kane and led him up and up through the dim galleries to his chamber, where again Shem locked his chains to the wall. Kane sat on his couch, chin on his fist, striving to find some motive in all the bizarre actions he had witnessed. And presently he realized that there was undue stir in the streets below.

The Englishman peered out from his window. Great fires blazed in the marketplace and the figures of men, curiously foreshortened, came and went. They seemed to be busying themselves about a figure in the center of the marketplace, but they clustered about it so thickly he could make nothing of it. A circle of soldiers ringed the group; the firelight glanced on their armor. About them clamored a disorderly mob, yelling and shouting.

Suddenly a scream of frightful agony cut through the din, and the shouting died away for an instant, to be renewed with more force than before. Most of the clamor sounded like protest, Kane thought, though mingled with it was the sound of jeers, taunting howls, and devilish laughter. And all through the babble rang those ghastly, intolerable shrieks.

A swift pad of naked feet sounded on the tiles, and the young slave who was called Sula rushed in and thrust his head into the window, panting with excitement. The firelight from without shone on his contorted face.

"The people strive with the spearmen," he exclaimed, forgetting in his excitement the order not to converse with the strange captive. "Many of the people loved well the young Prince Bel-lardath—oh, bwana, there was no evil in him! Why did you bid the king have him flayed alive?"

"I!" exclaimed Kane, taken aback and dumbfounded. "I said naught! I do not even know this prince! I have never seen him."

Sula turned his head and looked full into Kane's face.

"Now I know what I have secretly thought, bwana," he said in the Bantu tongue Kane understood. "You are no god, nor mouthpiece of a god, but a man such as I have seen before the men of Ninn took me captive. Once before, when I was small, I saw men cast in your mold, who came with their native servants and slew our warriors with weapons which spoke with fire and thunder."

"Truly I am but a man," answered Kane, dazedly. "But what—I do not understand. What is it they do in yonder marketplace?"

"They are skinning Prince Bel-lardath alive," answered Sula. "It has been talked freely among the marketplaces that the king and Yamen hated the prince, who is of the blood of Abdulai. But he had many followers among the people, especially among the Arbii, and not even the king dared sentence him to death. But when you were brought into the temple, secretly, none in the city knowing of it, Yamen said you were the mouthpiece of the gods. And he said Baal had revealed to him that Prince Bel-lardath had roused the wrath of the gods. So they brought him before the oracle of the gods—"

Kane swore sickly. How incredible—how ghastly—to think that his lusty English oaths had doomed a man to a horrible death. Aye—crafty Yamen had translated his random words in his own way. And so the prince, whom Kane had never seen before, writhed beneath the skinning knives of his executioners in the marketplace below, where the crowd shrieked or jeered.

"Sula," he said, "what do these people call themselves?"

"Assyrians, bwana," answered the slave absently, staring in horrified fascination at the grisly scene below.

III

In the days that followed Sula found opportunities from time to time to talk with Kane. Little he could tell the Englishman of the origin of the men of Ninn. He only knew that they had come out of the east in the long, long ago, and had built their massive city on the plateau. Only the dim legends of his tribe spoke of them. His people lived in the rolling plains far to the south and had warred with the people of the city for untold ages. His tribe was called Sulas, and they were strong and war-like, he said. From time to time they made raids on the Ninnites, and occasionally the Ninnites returned the raid, but not often did they venture far from the plateau. In such a raid Sula had been captured. Of late the Ninnites had been forced to range farther afield in search of slaves, as the tribes shunned the grim plateau, and generation by generation moved further back into the wilderness.

The life of a slave of Ninn was hard, Sula said, and Kane believed him—seeing the marks of lash, rack, and brand on the youth's body. The drifting ages had not softened the spirit of the Assyrians, nor modified their fierceness, a byword in the ancient East.

Kane wondered much at the presence of this ancient people in this unknown land, but Sula had nothing further to tell him. They came from the east, long, long ago—that was all Sula knew. The Englishman knew now why their features and language had seemed remotely familiar. Their features were the original Semitic features, now modified in the modern inhabitants of Mesopotamia, and many of their words had an unmistakable likeness to certain Hebraic words and phrases.

Kane learned from Sula that not all of the inhabitants were of one blood. They did not mix with their slaves, or if they did, the offspring of such a union was instantly put to death. The dominant strain, Sula had learned, was Assyrian; but there were some of the people, both commoners and nobles, who were called "Arbii." They were like the Assyrians, yet differing somewhat.

Another group were the "Kaldii"—magicians and soothsayers who were held in no great esteem by the true Assyrians. Shem, Sula said, and his kind were Elamites, and Kane started at the biblical term. There were not many of them, but they were the tools of the priests—slayers and doers of strange and unnatural deeds. Sula had suffered at the hands of Shem, as had every other slave of the temple.

And it was this same Shem on whom Kane kept hungry eyes riveted. At his girdle hung the golden key that meant liberty. But, as if he read the meaning in the Englishman's cold eyes, Shem walked with care, a dark sombre giant with a grim carven face. He came not within reach of the captive's long and steely arms, unless accompanied by armed guards.

Never a day passed but Kane heard the crack of the scourge, the screams of agonized slaves beneath the brand, the lash, or the skinning knife. Ninn was a veritable Hell, he reflected, ruled by the demoniac Asshur-ras-arab and his crafty and lustful satellite, Yamen the priest. The king was high priest as well, as had been his royal ancestors in ancient Nineveh. And Kane realized why they called him a Persian, seeing in him a resemblance to those wild old Aryan tribesmen who had ridden down from their mountains to sweep the Assyrian empire off the earth. Surely it was fleeing those yellow-haired conquerors that the people of Ninn had come into Africa.

The days passed and Kane abode as a captive in the city of Ninn. But he went no more to the temple as an oracle.

One day there was confusion in the city. Kane heard the trumpets blaring upon the wall, and the roll of kettle-drums. Steel clanged in the streets, and the sound of men marching rose to his eyrie. Looking out, over the wall, across the plateau, he saw a horde of naked black men approaching the city in loose formation. Their spears flashed in the sun, their headpieces of ostrich-plumes floated in the breeze, and their yells came faintly to him.

Sula rushed in, his eyes blazing.

"My people!" he exclaimed. "They come against the men of Ninn. My people are warriors! Bogaga is warchief—Katayo is king. The warchiefs of the Sulas hold their honors by the might of their hands, for any man who is strong enough to slay him with his naked hands, becomes warchief in his place! So Bogaga won the chieftainship, but it will be many a day before any slays him, for he is the mightiest chieftain of them all!"

Kane's window afforded a better view over the wall than any other, for his chamber was in the top-most tier of Baal's temple. To his chamber came Yamen, with his grim guards, Shem, and another sombre

Elamite. They stood out of Kane's reach, looking through one of the windows.

The mighty gates swung wide; the Assyrians were marching out to meet their enemies. Kane reckoned that there were fifteen hundred armed warriors; that left three hundred still in the city, the bodyguard of the king, the sentries, and house-troops of the various noblemen.

The host, Kane noted, was divided into four divisions. The center was in the advance, consisting of six hundred men, while each flank or wing was composed of three hundred. The remaining three hundred marched in compact formation behind the center, between the wings, so the whole presented an appearance of this figure:

The warriors were armed with javelins, swords, maces, and short heavy bows. On their backs were quivers bristling with shafts.

The Ninnites marched out on the plain in perfect order and took up their position apparently awaiting the attack. It was not slow in coming. Kane estimated that the attackers numbered at least three thousand warriors, and even at that distance he could appreciate their splendid stature and courage. But they had no system or order for warfare. It was in one great ragged, disorderly horde that they rushed onward, to be met by a withering blast of arrows that ripped through their bull-hide shields as though they had been made of paper.

The Assyrians had slung their shields about their necks and were drawing and loosing methodically, not in regular volleys as the archers of Crecy and Agincourt had loosed, but steadily and without pause, nevertheless. With reckless courage the Sulas hurled themselves forward, into the teeth of the fearful hail. Kane saw whole lines melt away, and the plain became carpeted with the dead. But the invaders came forward, wasting their lives like water. Kane marveled at the perfect discipline of the Semitic soldiers who went through their motions as coolly as if they were on the drill ground. The wings had moved forward, their foremost tips connecting with the ends of the center, presenting an unbroken front. The men in the company between the wings maintained their place, unmoving, not yet having taken any part in the battle.

The invading horde was broken, staggering back under the deadly fire against which flesh and blood could not stand. The great ragged crescent had broken to bits, and from the fire of the right flank and the center, the Sulas were falling back disorderly, hounded by the ranging shafts of the Ninnite warriors. But on the left flank, a frothing mob of perhaps four hundred savage fighters had burst through the fearful barrage and, yelling like fiends, they shocked against the Assyrian wing. But before the spears clashed, Kane saw the company in reserve between the wings wheel and march in double quick time to support the threatened wing. Against that double wall of six hundred mailed men of war, the onslaught staggered, broke, and reeled backward.

Swords flashed among the spears, and Kane saw the naked warriors falling like grain before the reaper as the javelins and swords of the Assyrians mowed them down. Not all the corpses on the bloody ground were those of the attackers, but where one Assyrian lay dead or wounded, ten Sulas had died.

Now the attackers were in full flight across the plain, and the iron ranks moved forward in quick but orderly pace, loosing at every step, hunting the vanquished across the plateau, plying the dagger on the wounded. They took no prisoners. Sulas did not make good slaves as Solomon was instantly to see.

In Kane's chamber, the watchers were crowded at the windows, eyes glued in fascination on the wild and gory scene. Sula's chest heaved with passion; his eyes blazed with the blood-lust of the savage as the shouts and the slaughter and the spears of his tribesmen fired all the slumbering ferocity in his warrior's soul.

With the yell of a blood-mad panther, he sprang on the backs of his masters. Before any could lift a hand, he snatched the dagger from Shem's girdle and plunged it to the hilt between Yamen's shoulders. The priest shrieked like a wounded woman and went to his knees, blood spurting, and the Elamites closed with the raging slave. Shem sought to seize his wrist, but the other Elamite and Sula whirled into a deadly embrace, plying their knives which were in an instant red to the hilt.

Eyes glaring, froth on their lips, they rolled and tumbled, slashing and stabbing. Shem, seeking to catch Sula's wrist, was struck by the hurtling bodies and knocked violently aside. He lost his footing and sprawled against Kane's couch.

Before he could move, the chained Englishman was on him like a great cat. At last the moment he had waited for had come! Shem was within his reach, and even as he sought to rise Kane's knee smote him in the breast, breaking his ribs. Kane's iron fingers locked in his throat. Solomon was scarcely aware of the terrible, wild-beast struggles of the Elamite who sought in vain to break that grasp. A red mist veiled the Englishman's sight and through it he saw horror growing in Shem's inhuman eyes—saw them distend and turn blood-shot—saw the mouth gape and the tongue protrude as the shaven head was bent back at a horrible angle; then Shem's neck snapped like a heavy branch and the straining body went limp in Kane's hands.

The Englishman snatched at the key in the dead man's girdle, and an instant later stood up free, feeling a wild surge of exultation sweep over him as he flexed his unhampered limbs. He glanced about the chamber. Yamen was gurgling out his life on the tiles, and Sula and the other Elamite lay dead, locked in each others' iron arms, literally slashed to pieces.

Kane ran swiftly from the chamber. He had no

plan except to escape from the temple he had grown to hate as a man hates Hell. He ran down the winding galleries, meeting no one. Evidently the servants of the temple had been massed on the walls watching the battle. But on the lower tier he came face to face with one of the temple guards. The man gaped at him stupidly—and Kane's fist crashed against his black-bearded jowl, stretching him senseless. Kane snatched up his heavy javelin. A thought had come to him that perhaps the streets would be deserted as the people watched the battle, and he could make his way across the city and scale the wall on the side next the lake.

He ran through the pillar-forested temple and out the mighty portal. There a scattering of people shrieked and fled at the sight of the strange figure emerging from the grim temple. Kane hurried down the street in the direction of the opposite gate, seeing but few people. Then as he turned into a side street, thinking to shorten his route, he heard a thunderous roar.

Ahead of him he saw four slaves bearing a richly ornamented litter such as nobles rode in. The occupant was a young girl whose jewel-bedecked garments showed her importance and wealth. And now around the corner came roaring a great, tawny shape. A lion, loose in the city streets!

The slaves dropped the litter and fled, shrieking, while the people on the housetops screamed. The girl cried out once, scrambling up in the very path of the charging monster. She stood facing it, frozen with terror.

Solomon Kane, at the first roar of the beast, experienced a fierce satisfaction. So hateful had Ninn become to him that the thought of a wild beast raging through its streets and devouring its cruel inhabitants had given the Puritan an indisputable satisfaction. But now, as he saw the pitiful figure of the girl facing the man-eater, he felt a pang of pity for her, and acted.

As the lion launched himself through the air, Kane hurled the javelin with all the power of his iron frame. Just behind the mighty shoulder it struck, transfixing the tawny body. A deafening roar burst from the beast which spun sidewise in mid-air, as though it had encountered a solid wall, and instead of the rending claws, it was the heavy, shaggy shoulder that smote the frail figure of its victim, hurling her aside as the great beast crashed to the earth.

Kane, forgetful of his own position, sprang forward and lifted the girl, trying to ascertain if she were injured. This was an easy task, since her garments, like the garments of most of the Assyrian noble women, were so scanty as to consist more of ornaments than of covering. Kane assured himself that she was only bruised and badly frightened.

He helped her to her feet, aware that a throng of curious onlookers surrounded him. He turned to press through them, and they made no effort to stop him. Suddenly a priest appeared and yelled something, pointing at him. The people instantly fell back, but half a dozen armored soldiers came forward, javelins ready. Kane faced the priest, fury seething in his soul. He was ready to leap among them and do what damage he could with his naked hands before he died, when down the stones of the street sounded the tramp of marching men. A company of warriors swung into view, their spears red from recent strife.

The girl cried out and ran forward to fling her arms about the stalwart neck of the young officer in command. There followed a rapid fire of conversation which Kane naturally could not understand. Then the officer spoke curtly to the guards who drew back. He advanced toward Kane, his empty hands outstretched, a smile on his lips. His manner was friendly in the extreme, and the Englishman realized that he was trying to express his gratitude for the rescue of the girl, who was no doubt either his sister or his sweetheart. The priest frothed and cursed, but the young noble answered him shortly, and made motions for Kane to accompany him. Then as the Englishman hesitated, suspicious, he drew his own sword and extended it to Kane, hilt foremost. Kane took the weapon; it might have been the form of courtesy to have refused it, but Kane was unwilling to take chances, and he felt much more secure with a weapon in his hand.

IV

Escorting Kane, the officer and his men marched quickly through the narrow streets. Their route was circuitous. Were they trying to bewilder Kane, or to ensure that the priest could not have them followed? Only the gift of the sword reassured the Englishman.

At last they halted, before a long house of baked brick, which Kane assumed to be the officer's home. The two-storyed house was built around a central courtyard. It had few windows, but the rooms were spacious. Indeed, they were almost bare apart from tables, stools, and a few wooden storage chests.

As soon as they entered the house, the bearing of the officer and of the young woman changed. They conferred in low voices, quickly and intensely. Was it only paranoia that made Kane sure they were discussing him? They reached agreement, and the officer dispatched his men on an errand. Again it was only the sword in his fist which reassured Kane.

Twilight was settling into the rooms. The girl moved about, lighting lamps, wicks protruding from pots of oil; her jewels glittering darkly as blood. She offered Kane a jug of wine, which he refused as courteously as he could without the help of words. He preferred to keep his wits clear. Her look made it evident that she desired him, and was accustomed to have what she desired. But he glanced indifferently at her scantily clad form, then met her gaze with the righteous stare of the Puritan. Rebuffed, she stalked angrily away.

The warriors returned singly, and reported to the

young officer—who, Kane noted, had fitted a new sword into his sheath. So Kane was to keep the one he held. From the officer's expression, the reports were favorable, but he seemed nonetheless impatient.

The girl moved among the warriors. It seemed not to be her purpose to inflame them, though some glanced at her with covert desire. Instead, she brought them to Kane to address him in various dialects. Eventually there came one who spoke Bantu.

Through the interpreter, the girl told Kane that her name was Siduri. The officer, her brother, was Labashi. Swiftly she drew from Kane an account of his adventures in the city. "We have brought you here to help you," she said when he had finished.

"Help me then to leave this city."

"We cannot. Already the men of King Asshur-rasarab have surrounded the city." She insisted on taking him up to the roof to show him. Myriad torches blazed on the city walls, which were crowded with figures; while from the center of the city a ring of torches spread out gradually, searching. Kane pointed out the latter, which was surely a more immediate threat. He felt restless and frustrated as a caged beast; a fury to use his sword, to hack his way out of Asshur, smoldered in him. But when they returned to the interpreter Siduri would say only: "We have a plan."

Was it his aloofness that made her determined to say no more? He was about to question Labashi when men began arriving at the house. It was evidently a secret meeting. Some of the men wore priestly robes, more austere than he had previously seen in Asshur. Others wore silk; he took them to be nobles. They were paler, and their bones more delicate, than the average men of the city. There were also several warriors—officers, by their bearing.

The dozen men conferred in low urgent tones, frequently glancing at Kane. Siduri attempted to join in the discussion, but most of the men ignored her, except for one young man, the tallest and most pale of them, who clearly knew and admired her.

Kane waited sombrely. He felt at the mercy of the discussion, and of Providence. The urge for tangible battle or action burned within him. Before he could voice his rage through the interpreter, the men seemed to reach a swift decision. "What have you decided?" Kane demanded.

It was Siduri who answered quickly. "You cannot leave the city while Asshur-ras-arab is king. You must help us overthrow him. Play the oracle for us, as you did for him."

Kane remembered the chains and the befuddling fumes. "I will not."

"There will be no risk. The Kaldii"—she indicated the priests—"have brewed a potion that will protect you from the effects of the drug. You will play the oracle, but you will know what you are doing."

Kane's spirit revolted. How could he assume the role of oracle of some heathen religion? "No," he said fiercely.

Uproar ensued, until Labashi calmed the conspirators. Then, despite the protests of Siduri and the tall young noble—whose name, Kane gathered, was Puzur—he explained the situation to Kane.

The officers, and many of the nobles, had grown sickened by the cruelty of Asshur-ras-arab. They had hoped that Prince Bel-lardath would lead them against the king—but the prince had been condemned by Yamen's interpretation of Kane's oracle.

Most of the warriors of Asshur who had died in today's battle had been Assyrians. Thus fate had favored the Kaldii and Arbii, and their supporters. But a civil war was likely to achieve only the destruction of Asshur. Now fate seemed to have aided the conspirators by delivering Kane to them. As oracle, he could indicate with unambiguous gestures that Asshur-ras-arab must relinquish the throne to Labashi, who was held in high regard by all the nobles.

Kane pondered. Though he had been drugged, he felt a pang of guilt for Bel-lardath's sufferings. Even if he managed to escape without aiding the conspirators, he would be leaving the city in the grip of a cruel king. Could Providence mean him to act the oracle? Had he been given this chance to make restitution for the bloodshed he had inadvertently caused?

Something else occurred to him. "What of the village whose people I followed here?"

"If any still live," Labashi vowed, "they will be set free."

There was a murmur of agreement. Kane could detect no guile in Labashi's voice. Perhaps he might be a good king—certainly he was to be preferred to Asshur-ras-arab. "Very well," Kane said at last, though reluctantly. "I will help you as best I can."

V

Kane felt curiously light-headed. A few minutes ago he had swallowed the drug prepared by the Kaldii. Its sweetish taste, not unpleasant, clung to his mouth. Only Labashi's apparent sincerity had persuaded Kane to entrust himself to the drug.

He was marching amid the conspirators, who were themselves surrounded by several dozen warriors, led by Labashi. Other companies of warriors paced them in the parallel streets, in case of ambush. As he was carried along by the rhythm of the march, Kane felt at the mercy of the situation. In order to play the oracle he had had to yield up his sword. Certainly Providence could not have deserted him—but the dark sullen buildings which cramped the streets oppressed him, while the presence of the drug in his mind made him feel trapped and vulnerable, almost possessed.

Labashi had sent messengers to all the nobles who were not involved in the conspiracy, announcing that the oracle would speak in the temple. Last of all he had sent a messenger to Asshur-ras-arab. By the time the king learned what was to happen, the nobles would be gathering in the temple.

Suddenly, at the end of the narrow street, two soldiers appeared, bearing torches: the king's men, searching for Kane. For a moment they faltered; then, overwhelmed by the odds, they fled. A murmur of jubilation passed through the warriors. Kane was reminded uneasily how young many of them were—not least the prospective king.

They had coached him in the gestures he must use as oracle. He must not speak, for speech could be misinterpreted. As he strode, he rehearsed the gestures in his mind, and at the same time prayed silently. "God of Hosts, let it be that I have interpreted Thy purpose correctly. If I am walking an evil path, and have strayed from Thy way by presuming to know Thy will, give me a sign."

No sign came, and the march continued unabated. Soon the street was blocked by the hulk of the temple. Beneath its tiers that mounted toward the blackly overclouded sky, the torches borne by the company seemed small as matches. The great bulk loomed over Kane like a gigantic squatting demon, overpowering as the night's heat. Against the thick sky the tiers, reared toward heaven, seemed to totter.

Reluctantly Kane strode with the rest of the company into the maw of the temple. As the torchlight flickered over the massive wall, the marching carved figures appeared to stir, as did the figures—lions with human faces, human bodies with inhuman heads—that stared from the pillars. To Kane's bewildered senses it was as though the figures had awakened to ward off the intrusion.

At last the company neared the central space. In his throne opposite the idol sat Asshur-ras-arab, his face grim and cruel as that of the stone colossus. Among the pillars behind him Kane saw the glint of many fire-lit javelins. His warriors were assembled there.

Opposite him, outside the circular space, stood the nobles in their shining robes. They turned nervously as the newcomers approached. Their faces betrayed their doubts, and Kane felt a responsive pang. But Labashi gestured the nobles not to falter, and some of them seemed heartened.

His warriors formed a semicircle among the pillars, opposite the king's men. Two remained, guarding the Englishman. This was to show that he was reluctant, the better to impress the nobles with his oracle. But the sense that the warriors' swords were turned against him made him feel restless and vulnerable.

Labashi strode to the edge of the space. He bowed, plainly more as a ritual than as a tribute. The king watched him like a great snake; firelight flicked toward the young officer, like the tongues of reptiles.

Labashi began to speak. His voice was strong, almost imperious. Amid his words Kane heard the name of Bel-lardath. The king waited, patient as stone, though to Kane the speech had the sound of a sentence of death. Labashi indicated the nobles, who nodded uneasy agreement. If they were questioning the king's fitness to rule, they did so timidly.

The king spoke, briefly and coldly. At once Labashi turned and pointed at Kane, then looked to the nobles, whose agreement was audible now, though still timid. He had called for the oracle.

Kane grew tense. If the king commanded his men to deal with the upstart, he would be left unarmed in the midst of a battle. But Asshur-ras-arab nodded slowly, with a cruel smile, and beckoned two warriors to conduct Kane to the oracle's throne.

What reason had the king to smile so? Labashi's confidence was clearly faltering, but he could hardly withdraw his call for the oracle. The men led Kane into the vast stone space.

A priest emerged from the shadows, bearing the green silken robe. He was fatter than Yamen; his oily face glistened and quivered like quicksand. He looked weak and corrupt. Kane was made to sit, then the priest spread the robe over him. But before his wrists and ankles could be locked to the throne, Labashi shouted something.

The shout took one soldier unawares; he dropped a shackle, which clanked loudly. Now its existence could not be denied. The king's face darkened. After a short and bitter discussion, interrupted by murmurs from the nobles, he allowed Kane's arms to be left free, though his ankles were shackled.

Perhaps the plot would succeed. But Kane felt as though he had been tricked into deviltry. The soldiers withdrew, leaving him in the power of the swollen priest. The king smiled cruelly. Again the Puritan offered up a silent prayer.

Asshur-ras-arab raised his golden wand and struck the gong. He gazed at the nobles with open contempt as they prostrated themselves before him, and gloated over the sight of their fawning for some time before speaking the word that released them. He gazed challengingly at Labashi's furious eyes, then motioned the priest to begin.

The priest advanced toward Kane. As the light from the brazier licked his face, his jowls looked as though they were melting. He commenced his wailing chant, and cast a handful of powder into the flames.

The fumes billowed thickly into Kane's face. He retched; the smell and taste seemed stronger, more acrid. But his head remained clear. Though his skull felt weightless, the fumes had not clouded his mind.

But the priest was still chanting. A second handful of the drug hissed in the flames, and a third. Kane was almost blinded by the clouds that poured into his face. He glimpsed the secret smiles of the king and the priest. They knew, or at least suspected, that an antidote had been prepared; and they planned to overcome it by increasing the strength of the drug.

And they seemed to have succeeded. Kane's head reeled. His eyes could focus on nothing; pillars and men grew dim. They were moving sluggishly around him, as though the entire temple had begun to spin.

Everything quivered as though glimpsed through water.

Oaths struggled within his lips. But some part of his mind held steady; he knew he must not speak. He ground his teeth, and blood trickled rustily between them. Ahead of him, amid the slow blurred dance of the pillars, he saw a glowing figure on a massive throne. He must point at that figure; he had rehearsed the gesture. His hand felt heavy as the temple, but it managed to grope into the air. At last he succeeded in pointing.

Still the fumes hung about his face. The acrid taste seemed to have spread into the fabric of his skull. What must he do now? He remembered eventually—he was to make a sign of casting out, raising his fists then flinging their emptiness away, toward the figure.

With an effort that made the temple sway, he raised his fists. Then, exhausted by the strain that the noxious drug imposed, they opened feebly. They were capable of no more—and they were raised in an attitude of worship, not of rejection, toward the man on the throne.

Kane heard a subdued dismayed murmuring. Men were bemoaning his failure. He had betrayed them. The last conscious fragment of the soul that was Solomon Kane writhed in self-disgust. His hands convulsed—and flung their empty revulsion toward the throne.

At once he heard cries of triumph. Labashi knocked aside the brazier, and Kane's vision cleared a little. He glimpsed the priest retreating, brandishing his scourge to ward off any attack. The nobles were advancing on the throne where Asshur-ras-arab sat, frowning like granite. When Labashi addressed the king there was no mistaking his tone of command.

The king rose to his feet. He pointed at Kane, and his face writhed with fury. His beard bristled like an animal's pelt; his eyes shone with rage. Abruptly he descended from his throne, thrusting the nobles aside.

Seizing a sword from one of them, who still dared not struggle with him, he bore down on Kane.

There came a general murmur of disapproval. Clearly he was threatening to commit sacrilege. The nobles converged on him—but they were not swift enough, and Kane could not struggle aside. It was one of his own warriors who threw the javelin that impaled the king and emerged from his chest amid a gush of blood. He fell dead before the inhuman idol, like a sacrifice.

Kane's mind was clearing. He recalled what he had undertaken to do. Lifting his enfeebled arm, he pointed at Labashi, then with both hands made a gesture of raising him to the throne. Amid cries of approval, two nobles placed the golden circlet on Labashi's head, and the wand in his hands.

Before Labashi would ascend the throne, he stooped to release Kane. As he did so, Kane saw the girl Siduri and the pale noble Puzur conferring hurriedly and secretly. Kane stood up, stumbling a little, and saluted the new king. Then he made for the warrior who spoke Bantu, to demand a place to rest.

But Siduri blocked his way. "You must not leave us," she said through the interpreter. "We may need your powers again. You are our oracle."

She saw him as a means to further her ambitions. No doubt she intended to make use of him as it appeared she had of Puzur. If he refused her, would she go so far as to betray the plot, her brother's ruse? Kane had seen ambition cause worse betrayals.

But he did not hesitate. "No," he said. "I have done all that I was required to do."

Labashi was being ushered to the throne by the nobles. As he sat, he muttered a command. The interpreter said to Kane, "The king bids you go free."

Siduri must have found the frustration of this new rebuff unbearable; it must have seemed to quash all her ambitions. Fury inflamed her eyes. Drawing a dagger, she rushed at Kane. Labashi shouted a command. But she writhed between the soldiers who tried to seize her, and came on.

Puzur leaped at her from the side. Horror twisted his face. Was he appalled by this new threat of sacrilege, or by her apparent intention to spoil their plot and to dash his ambitions? Perhaps he was unsure of his impulse himself—but his sword cut the girl down, cleaving her neck.

He dropped the bloody sword and stood gazing at the corpse of Siduri. He was shivering; his eyes grew vacant. The temple was silent, except for the footsteps of Labashi, descending from his throne.

The king knelt by his sister. When at last he rose, the crimson rage in his eyes had been doused by resigned sadness. He waved Puzur away brusquely, but stayed the warriors who would have pursued him. Kane thought that the young man might have it in him to be a king. In time, silent warriors bore the girl's body away into the depths of the temple. Labashi followed, head bowed.

That night Kane slept in the house where Labashi had lived. He slept on a wooden bed with blankets, for the first time in many nights. Two warriors guarded him from any intrusion.

Next day, however, when he walked unmolested through the gates of Asshur, he was glad to leave the city. He knew that men's souls could change, and that many would rather find a scapegoat for evil than take the blame themselves. Before he had reached the edge of the plateau, the sounds of the city were inaudible. He descended the cliff road and made his way across the savannas. When he looked back, the city was invisible. He felt as though he had wakened from a dream of Assyria; and he had a curious inkling that the world beyond the plateau would never hear of the city again. He turned away, and set his face toward the outer world.

SOLOMON KANE'S HOMECOMING

*The white gulls wheeled above the cliffs, the air was
  slashed with foam,
The long tides moaned along the strand when Solomon Kane came home.
He walked in silence strange and dazed through the
  little Devon town,
His gaze, like a ghost's come back to life, roamed up
  the streets and down.*

*The people followed wonderingly to mark his spectral
  stare,
And in the tavern silently they thronged about him
  there.
He heard as a man hears in a dream the worn old
  rafters creak,
And Solomon lifted his drinking-jack and spoke as a
  ghost might speak:*

*"There sat Sir Richard Grenville once; in smoke and
  flame he passed,
"And we were one to fifty-three, but we gave them
  blast for blast.
"From crimson dawn to crimson dawn, we held the
  Dons at bay.
"The dead lay littered on our decks, our masts were
  shot away.*

*"We beat them back with broken blades, till crimson
  ran the tide;
"Death thundered in the cannon smoke when Richard
  Grenville died.
"We should have blown her hull apart and sunk
  beneath the Main."*

*The people saw upon his wrists the scars of the racks
of Spain.*

*"Where is Bess?" said Solomon Kane. "Woe that I
caused her tears."*

*"In the quiet churchyard by the sea she has slept these
seven years."*

The sea-wind moaned at the window-pane, and Solomon bowed his head.

*"Ashes to ashes and dust to dust, and the fairest fade,"
he said.*

His eyes were mystical deep pools that drowned unearthly things,

*And Solomon lifted up his head and spoke of his
wanderings.*

*"Mine eyes have looked on sorcery in the dark and
naked lands,*

*"Horror born of the jungle gloom and death on the
pathless sands.*

*"And I have known a deathless queen in a city old
as Death,*

"Where towering pyramids of skulls her glory witnesseth.

*"Her kiss was like an adder's fang, with the sweetness
Lilith had,*

*"And her red-eyed vassals howled for blood in that
City of the Mad.*

*"And I have slain a vampire shape that sucked a black
king white,*

*"And I have roamed through grisly hills where dead
men walked at night.*

*"And I have seen heads fall like fruit in the slaver's
barracoon,*

*"And I have seen winged demons fly all naked in the
moon.*

*"My feet are weary of wandering and age comes on
apace;*

"I fain would dwell in Devon now, forever in my place,"
The howling of the ocean pack came whistling down the gale,
And Solomon Kane threw up his head like a hound that sniffs the trail.

A-down the wind like a running pack the hounds of the ocean bayed,
And Solomon Kane rose up again and girt his Spanish blade.
In his strange cold eyes a vagrant gleam grew wayward and blind and bright,
And Solomon put the people by and went into the night.

A wild moon rode the wild white clouds, the waves in white crests flowed,
When Solomon Kane went forth again and no man knew his road.
They glimpsed him etched against the moon, where clouds on hilltop thinned;
They heard an eery echoed call that whistled down the wind.

ABOUT THE AUTHOR

ROBERT ERVIN HOWARD was born in the small town of Cross Plains, Texas, in 1906. His first story, "Spear and Fang," was published when he was eighteen, in *Weird Tales*. Over the next twelve years, Howard wrote over a million words of fantasy, Westerns, pirate yarns, detective and adventure stories for the pulp magazines. He is best known for his larger-than-life heroes: King Kull, Solomon Kane, Bran Mak Morn, and the greatest hero of them all, Conan, who swagger through exotic and far-off lands and times having fabulous adventures, conquering kingdoms and beautiful women with equal ease. Howard committed suicide on June 11, 1936, when he heard his mother had lapsed into a terminal coma.

THE WORLD OF ROBERT E. HOWARD

Born and bred in the rough, raw days just after the west was tamed, this country doctor's son lived out his short but amazing life in the small town of Cross Plains, Texas. Robert Ervin Howard, big and burly, was secretly a dreamer and a poet—a true pioneer in his own way.

A prolific writer of fiction, Howard struggled to gain recognition, writing for the pulp magazines that flourished in the 1920s and 30s. He ultimately became known as the leading American writer of heroic fantasy. His admirers included H. P. Lovecraft, Clark Ashton Smith and August Derleth.

Howard created his own world. A realm peopled with primitive men, barbarians, warriors, wizards, strong, beautiful women, and worshippers of dark gods in the forgotten lost civilizations. His heroes—CONAN, SOLOMON KANE and KULL—are all larger than life, believing in direct action, yet at the prey of emotional forces they can't control. Howard's stories are well known for strong plots, a colorful and vivid writing style, a marvelous sense of pace and action, and an emotional intensity that sweeps the reader along.

Howard's short life ended in suicide in 1936. However in 1951, a pile of unsold manuscripts was discovered. Arrangements were made with his heirs for their publication. Then much later, another batch of unpublished stories were found. Now, here are a number of those stories, many of them published in paperback for the first time.

For those who yearn for far-off and fanciful kingdoms of high adventure, of daring deeds and daring men who counter cunning with courage and conquer evil at any cost, read the stories of Robert E. Howard.

KULL

King of Valusia, he held the throne against plotting noblemen, priests of an overthrown serpent god and sorcerers who sought to topple this brawny barbarian. Combining mystery and splendor, wonder and horror, this book recounts Kull's adventures in the Forbidden Lake and among the eerily strange inhabitants of the Enchanted Land. (Available September)

SOLOMON KANE I: SKULLS IN THE STARS

The amazing exploits of the swashbuckling hero of the 16th century. Kane, who has the great courage to trust his instincts, is forever in pursuit of evil. This time the tumultuous trail takes him from England to a politically seething France, darkest Africa, and finally to the dangerous denizens of the Black Forest. (Available December)

SOLOMON KANE II: THE HILLS OF THE DEAD

Solomon's newest adventures in pursuit of evil lead him to the exotic jungles of the west coast of Africa. There, he encounters vampirism, meets an old sea-faring friend, finds the city of the unhumans, and ultimately discovers the survivors of an ancient civilization. (Available Feb. 1979)

(Look for all of these Robert Howard books, as well as the Conan adventures. Available from Bantam Books, wherever paperbacks are sold.)

OUT OF THIS WORLD!

That's the only way to describe Bantam's great series of science fiction classics. These space-age thrillers are filled with terror, fancy and adventure and written by America's most renowned writers of science fiction. Welcome to outer space and have a good trip!

☐	11392	**STAR TREK: THE NEW VOYAGES 2** by Culbreath & Marshak	$1.95
☐	11945	**THE MARTIAN CHRONICLES** by Ray Bradbury	$1.95
☐	12753	**STAR TREK: THE NEW VOYAGES** by Culbreath & Marshak	$1.95
☐	11502	**ALAS BABYLON** by Pat Frank	$1.95
☐	12180	**A CANTICLE FOR LEIBOWITZ** by Walter Miller, Jr.	$1.95
☐	12673	**HELLSTROM'S HIVE** by Frank Herbert	$1.95
☐	12454	**DEMON SEED** by Dean R. Koontz	$1.95
☐	12044	**DRAGONSONG** by Anne McCaffrey	$1.95
☐	11599	**THE FARTHEST SHORE** by Ursula LeGuin	$1.95
☐	11600	**THE TOMBS OF ATUAN** by Ursula LeGuin	$1.95
☐	11609	**A WIZARD OF EARTHSEA** by Ursula LeGuin	$1.95
☐	12005	**20,000 LEAGUES UNDER THE SEA** by Jules Verne	$1.50
☐	11417	**STAR TREK XI** by James Blish	$1.50
☐	12655	**FANTASTIC VOYAGE** by Isaac Asimov	$1.95
☐	02517	**LOGAN'S RUN** by Nolan & Johnson	$1.75

Buy them at your local bookstore or use this handy coupon for ordering:

Bantam Books, Inc., Dept. SF, 414 East Golf Road, Des Plaines, Ill. 60016

Please send me the books I have checked above. I am enclosing $_____ (please add 75¢ to cover postage and handling). Send check or money order —no cash or C.O.D.'s please.

Mr/Mrs/Miss_____

Address_____

City_____ State/Zip_____

SF—2/79

Please allow four weeks for delivery. This offer expires 8/79.

THE EXCITING REALM OF STAR TREK

☐	2151	**STAR TREK LIVES!** by Lichtenberg, Marshak & Winston	$1.95
☐	12753	**STAR TREK: THE NEW VOYAGES** by Culbreath & Marshak	$1.95
☐	11392	**STAR TREK: THE NEW VOYAGES 2** by Culbreath & Marshak	$1.95
☐	10159	**SPOCK, MESSIAH! A Star Trek Novel** by Cogswell & Spano	$1.75
☐	10978	**THE PRICE OF THE PHOENIX** by Marshak & Culbreath	$1.75
☐	11145	**PLANET OF JUDGMENT** by Joe Haldeman	$1.75

THRILLING ADVENTURES IN INTERGALACTIC SPACE

BY JAMES BLISH

☐	12591	SPOCK MUST DIE!	$1.75
☐	12589	STAR TREK 1	$1.75
☐	10811	STAR TREK 2	$1.50
☐	12312	STAR TREK 3	$1.75
☐	12311	STAR TREK 4	$1.75
☐	12325	STAR TREK 5	$1.75
☐	11697	STAR TREK 6	$1.50
☐	10815	STAR TREK 7	$1.50
☐	12731	STAR TREK 8	$1.75
☐	12111	STAR TREK 9	$1.75
☐	11992	STAR TREK 10	$1.75
☐	11417	STAR TREK 11	$1.50
☐	11382	STAR TREK 12	$1.75

Buy them at your local bookstore or use this handy coupon for ordering:

Bantam Books, Inc., Dept. ST, 414 East Golf Road, Des Plaines, Ill. 60016

Please send me the books I have checked above. I am enclosing $_____ (please add 75¢ to cover postage and handling). Send check or money order—no cash or C.O.D.'s please.

Mr/Mrs/Miss_____

Address_____

City_____State/Zip_____

ST—2/79

Please allow four weeks for delivery. This offer expires 8/79.